They All Die At The End

Peter Tarnofsky

Also by Peter Tarnofsky:

Timestand
Benny Baker

They All Die At The End

Peter Tarnofsky

A brief word about the title: Many years ago, before I was old enough to know better, my standard answer to anyone asking my opinion of a film (or play, or book, or television programme) was to say that "they all die at the end" – irrespective, obviously, of the actual outcome. On at least one memorable occasion, I was accused of ruining the ending – and for a film I had not even seen. Generally, however, friends and acquaintances realised that this answer did not constitute a spoiler – until now. N.B. I no longer give my opinion of films in this way.

First published in Great Britain in 2011.

First edition.

ISBN 978 1 4476 6485 7

for Liz – and anyone else who always wants to know how it's going to turn out before they begin

Contents

Yellow Banana Smile

It was the banana that got him in the end.

All those desperately well-meaning friends in their expensive skiing jackets with their self-satisfied bleating that the cigarettes would lead to a long, painful, hacking early death – they were all wrong. It was the banana, his little joke, sitting there plotting his demise as it gradually turned green to yellow to brown to black.

He didn't see their faces as the back swung out and the front swung in – the faces of the children he would never have with the woman he had never met. Even at the end, his imagination failed him, serving him up bland blurred featureless unborn children to mourn – or to mourn him.

The Marlboro Lights used to rattle around on the ciggie-shelf, as he called it, the ridiculous cubby-hole with its recessed speedometer. He'd always smoked Marlboro Lights – never touched anything else – he just liked the way it sounded when he asked for it in the little shop around the corner. 'Marlboro', with its lazily truncated American spelling – he liked saying the word – and 'Light' was his concession to healthy living – that and the soon to lapse gym membership which was an expensive way to sit in a steam room once a month. He'd considered putting another packet next to it but thought they'd rattle off each other so he bought a banana, good nutritious food, and wedged it in. The banana will absorb some of the toxins, he'd tell anyone whether they asked or not. Make me live longer. But all the time it was plotting.

Sally had lost interest in him but, yet again, there she was. He had read that, in some parts of the world, the slang for passenger seat was 'seat of death'. Sally was either fearless or unaware of this – he suspected the latter as Sally was not well-read or well-travelled – or well-heeled for that matter. He had read that, in the final reckoning – no matter the love, the duty, the sacrificial wish – instinct always led the driver to swerve to his own advantage, or what instinct would perceive as selfish advantage.

Each time he reached down for the packet, his hand found the banana first. He'd tried putting the banana on the left (just remember that the banana should be left on the shelf) but, while avoiding the double-parkers, the wrong-way parkers, the death-wish pedestrians, the shrieking wrong-side ambulances, the way-over-the-centre-line juggernauts, instinct took over and his left hand went to the left. He'd tried putting it on the right (just remember the banana looks like a pen to write with) but by then he was remembering that the banana should be left on the shelf. He'd tried taking both off the shelf and just putting the cigarette packet back where it felt natural – except it felt natural in the middle and then he couldn't get the banana in at all. He'd tried reaching where he felt the cigarettes wouldn't be – but on those occasions, he was right and they weren't.

His friends weren't returning his calls as quickly as they used to. He hadn't seen Robert since that time last month when he'd walked into the lounge and asked what was different, he was sure something was different, that he'd changed the furniture, the curtains, moved the bookcase – but no, Robert had said, nothing. It was then he realised that the room felt smaller, he'd honestly felt it used to be bigger and he tried saying it as a joke but Robert didn't laugh and both of them realised that he hadn't been there for so long that his memory of the room had stretched and distorted. They'd had a good laugh that night but he was sure there had been a sneer when Robert had unlocked the balcony for him to go out for a smoke. No zealot like a convert, someone had once told him, but it was only on that night that he'd understood what it meant.

No, Robert couldn't have them in the house any more, not with the little one, and he'd bravely and brazenly given up, shown that his will-power was up to the task. He hadn't flinched once, no relapses. Smug bastard. And now he was rushing home after work to spend time with Jake or Jack or Zac or whatever the hell the child's name was, no time for standing outside the local for a pint and a smoke any more. Instead, Robert was cutting out bits of photos from some glossy magazine – cars and houses and flowers and anything colourful – while the boy, tongue out with concentration, rubbed Pritt over the backs (and the table) and jammed them down on a sheet of paper already crumpling under the sludge of glue and infant thumb pressure. It was a collage. How lovely. You'd have thought the two of them were creating great art instead of just a load of rubbish stuck onto cheap photocopier paper. He's done seven of them already, said Robert proudly.

Maybe he'd feel differently, hell maybe he'd set up his own nursery (as if, given his background), once he had a child. It wasn't going to be with Sally though. He was recognising the signs. Probably happen tonight, although it might drag on till the weekend – depending on whether she had a date with anyone else for Saturday. If she did, he'd get the "it's not you, it's me" tonight. Otherwise he'd have to give the speech on Saturday – probably after dinner, perhaps later – depends how much she had to drink and how strong his grip on his morals turned out to be that night.

There didn't seem to be as many fish left in his sea these days, so he had to make the most of whatever he could catch – at least that was how he justified it to himself – after all, they weren't throwing themselves at him the way they used to.

He blamed his hair. It had done him proud –
outlasted plenty of his friends', gave him no small
pleasure to see their scalps gradually brightening
around the backs of their heads while he still had
plenty to run his fingers through. But it was giving
up on him now, and quickly. Three times he'd set
off for Vince's, to get the whole lot chopped down
to grade two or whatever, but he'd lost his nerve and
gone to the newsagent for a red-top instead. Other
than the hair, he could pass for thirty-ish, blame the
lines on the fags and colourful life although, truth
be told, there had been plenty of the former and
pretty much none of the latter.

He'd miss Beth. No he wouldn't. He'd miss
having somewhere indoors where he could smoke
with someone else. The conversation was rubbish
but he'd gradually worked his way through her
friends and, now that he was one or two dates away
from dumping Sally, he wasn't sure he could face
her again. It had been bad enough when he'd sworn
at Mandy's four year old after the little bastard
walked in on them – obviously that had been it for
him and Mandy but he'd managed to wheedle and
whine his way back onto Beth's sofa. He'd miss her
– she was his mate, not in that way – he'd never
fancied her but he'd caught her looking at him – he
snorted, in your dreams love, wouldn't be seen with
that. He wouldn't miss her. Just didn't enjoy the
smoking without the talking, the ash sometimes
hanging, sometimes dropping as his hand waved

and rolled in time with the words. He didn't need the talking – just the company as he made smoke rings at the daytime television couch jockeys. He couldn't make smoke rings anyway – he'd get by.

Sally was just sitting there – staring straight ahead. He was just driving – no idea where, he'd said he wanted to surprise her and she'd just shrugged but he hadn't had anything in mind and now he was just going, just to move, just to look like he had a plan but wishing that the traffic would get worse, would slow to a stop, maybe those traffic lights could go out and that learner three cars in front would never have the nerve to pull out so they'd just have to sit there and, after a while, he could say there was no point now and he'd have to save the surprise for another time and how about they just went to the pub. His fingers were twitching, he reached through the steering wheel for the Marlboros but found the banana. He shoved it back, swore under his breath. Sally didn't even look round.

She didn't know because he hadn't told her and he hadn't told her because she would have given him a pitying look and told him that she could have seen it coming a mile off. He had lost his job two weeks ago. The company was being downsized or rightsized or they just didn't want him there – didn't make any difference to him. He'd wanted to go but he'd wanted to go to somewhere, not to nowhere and even though he'd felt delighted that he'd been given that kick up the backside to go out there and find something better where he'd be appreciated, the delight had seemed so thin and so hollow and had shattered away leaving him able but unwilling to spend all day in bed – he'd always liked being active, into work early, getting stuck in with as many meetings as would have him, being vocal and vociferous and opinionated and argumentative and he supposed it wasn't surprising that his boss had moved from respecting him to reprimanding him when he'd told another team to stop being so obstructive in fairly strong language and with the senior manager in the room. No, he wasn't sorry and yes, he would do it again if it shook them up so they would sort their ideas out and so, there it was, a verbal warning on his file. It was a small step from reprimanding him to hating his guts and so, with the statutory minimum, he was out.

The criminal record obviously wasn't going to help his job applications and he did not have high hopes for an offsetting reference from the old firm.

He had been so young at the time, his mid-twenties – practically still a child. Law-abiding, diligent, caring, clean-living – all the words, so many words spun by his barrister and yet still guilty but at least not taken down, at least a suspended sentence. Two years off the road, two years of buses and taxis and lifts from friends. The rest of his life with insurance expensive enough to give him a nosebleed. The rest of his life seeing that limp, twisted, bloodied thing that used to be someone's hopes and dreams and reason for living and was now, was now, was now cold. It was the father's fault, it was the mother's fault, it couldn't be his fault, he was only doing twenty-five, he was watching the road because he could see the kids playing on the other side and he knew what they were like but he didn't see that couple had a kid because of the parked cars and no one expects an adult to run out into the road and he didn't see their kid, their unrestrained unwatched kid, so he was watching the other side and then that sound as it went up and that other sound as it went down and then the screaming which he still hears every night. The screaming went on and on and on and he wished it would stop as he sat in the car and he didn't even turn off the engine and it was only when the policeman banged on the door that he realised the screaming was coming from him.

His own father told him to take up smoking. You need something for when the trembling starts, he said, watery eyes looking near him or around him but now so rarely at him. But eat plenty of fruit to make up for it, he said, trying to be jovial. Jovial – that's a word not used so much any more, and normally to talk about old people. Young people aren't jovial – it's not trendy. Like the way young people can be lithe but old people have to settle for sprightly.

He doesn't see the kid in his dreams but he hears

that sound as it went up and that other sound as it went down. He hears the sounds in the closing of a car door, in the putting the pint glasses back on the bar, in the slamming of the supermarket trolley back into its rack, even in the way Sally drums her fingers on the dashboard. His fingers start twitching. She's got something on her mind all right but she's saving it for when she can get more mileage out of it. She's saving it for when his surprise turns out to be a big disappointment – it'll be the dreary icing on her disappointment cake. She's probably hoping it rains too, a depressingly British steady drizzle, to help make her point about how he's wasted her life, wasted the proud tick and tock of her biological clock and how she's not getting back the days she's spent with him or some obtuse cliché like that.

Maybe he should just park right now, tell her it's over, drive her home and move on. That would save him the bother of listening to her little speech. Oh Christ she's started to talk.

She's not looking at him and the preamble is making him want to gnaw his fingernails or shout at her to get to the point. Apparently she feels really awkward with what she's about to say. Big deal. And she wanted to wait till they got wherever it was they were going but she's decided she might as well say what she wants to say now. Great – save him some petrol. And she hopes this won't come as a surprise to him. Not likely, although he's surprised she's saying it now – must have a hot date lined up with someone else.

Finally she looks him in the eye. They're waiting for traffic lights so he can look at her. He's using his unreadable steely gaze but he finds it hard to keep the eye contact because she's blinking nervously and telling him she'd like him to move in because she thinks they've got to that stage seeing as how it's three years now and he's renting and always said he hated his flat but that he'd have to smoke outside. And she loves him.

No one has ever said anything like this to him before in his life. He wants to smile, a thin sad smile, and tell her how much she means to him (without saying how little that is) but that he's not ready and that he is confused and that he needs a break to sort out his head. But she caught him off guard so he grins and says he'd love to and they kiss then the guy behind hoots because the lights have turned green and the car in front must be at least a hundred yards away. He finds himself thinking how patient the hooting driver must have been before he remembers that he's just agreed to move in with Sally.

Aren't women supposed to have intuition, he's asking himself and would try to remember to ask Robert if he saw him again before too long had passed. She certainly can't read me, he thought, feeling both proud of his ability to pretend love and affection, while feeling appalled at the way the evening had turned out. He reached for the cigarettes and found the banana. He flipped it over, turning its yellow frown into a black smile. The dashboard lights must have been gently cooking it, he thought, turning the yellow side back round to the front.

He moves his hand sideways to the cigarettes, just to check they're there, gives the packet a shake to hear the rattle (at least five left), then replaces it. He doesn't want one – well, he does but he doesn't want the lecture that would come with it – just needs the reassurance that they're easily to hand, right in front of him, a comfort that won't let him down. Well, it won't let him down until the long, painful, hacking early death – but he'll worry about that when he gets there. Anyway, something else will probably get him first (it will), something that comes out of nowhere or something right in front of him which he can see but can't do anything about. She's still looking at him, waiting for him to say something else but he wasn't listening to what she just said so just smiles and grunts and pretends to be driving carefully.

Has it really been three years? Have they really had seven holidays together without even counting a few long weekend bargain flight European cities? Was it him who had kissed her mother and shaken hands with her father and held her in the steady drizzle as they lowered her grandmother into the ground, the umbrella discarded inside-out only a few paces from the chapel? Are they his clothes, his toothbrush, his books, his photographs already festooned around her cupboards, her shelves, her walls and her floors?   Sleepwalking, all of it, meaningless to him now and yet the path of least resistance, that vicious hoary old cliché, is pulling him into a deeper and wider and, damn it, longer relationship with her. He might as well put the ring on her finger and noose around his own neck. He smiles a resigned, weary smile.

What are you smiling about – she wants to know. He rummages through their shared history for something harmless – the cake! The cake, she nods, smiles, nearly laughs. Her niece Jenny, or maybe she's her cousin or a friend's daughter – or was her name Janine? He doesn't know, he doesn't care. It was her eleventh or eighth or fifteenth birthday party and her idiot father wanted a photograph of his little angel with her birthday cake which he'd bought – all ballerinas and television programme tie-in – so he's there, doing the dad-photographer crouch, flash angled up to bounce off the ceiling, the eye squint, the knee bounce, the left a bit, the tip it forward a bit, the tip it forward a bit more. He never found out whether the idiot father cut his losses and took photographs anyway of his little angel caked with icing, crying into the wreckage as it oozed and crumbled and stained the new carpets.

He knows no one would do that with their wedding cake. There will be no wedding cake, there will be no wedding but he will be moving into her place unless he can find a way out – there must be a way out, somewhere, hidden – but he was always good at finding. A way out with head held high and honour satisfied and no more pain for Sally than she deserves which is a little, for blindsiding him like that, but not too much, because she's a decent human being even though he only wanted to see her once, or maybe twice, more in his life and even though she's a conniving, devious little bitch for getting him to agree to move in with her instead of dumping him like she was supposed to do.

He's got it. He'll tell her he's lost his job. She'll start sympathetic, quickly move into 'I told you so' and some sanctimonious work-ethic twaddle and end up cross with him which he can then work up into a row and she'll tell him to take her home and he'll drive there in stony silence and that, dear Sally, will be that. She can chuck out the stuff he's left at her place – he's not bothered.

Here we go. He uses the line about having to tell her something – but she's not listening because she's seen some kids playing outside a house, and she's stiffened, and she keeps looking at them, then looking at him to check he's seen them, then looking back, like she's going to grab the steering wheel or yank on the handbrake at the slightest provocation – or the slightest appearance of driving without due care and attention. And he wants to smile and say it's okay, he's seen them and he's only doing thirty, but instead he is just so angry – angry at her for the unspoken accusation that he's only a hairbreadth from doing it again, angry at himself for telling her about his history, angry at that limp, twisted, bloodied thing, angry at that ridiculous yellow banana smiling up at him, a false front hiding a blackened and rotten core.

He can't take it out on her. He wouldn't take it out on himself till later. But the banana could go, right now, straight out the window. He winds it down – what are you doing? He reaches through to grab the fruit. His hand finds the cigarettes. He shoves them back and gropes too hard for the banana. Putrid fruit flesh squirts down the dashboard, into his lap, probably some on his shoes, his new, suede-effect loafers – that wouldn't come out without a lot of trouble. He glances down to see the extent of the damage.

It's not 'look out': it's a guttural screech from Sally as one of the stupid children who'd been balancing on the kerb tips backwards and puts a foot out for balance, which goes into a pothole and over he goes and Sally grabs at the steering wheel and gives it a harsh wrench away from the child but the wheel spokes catch on his arm, which is still holding the stinking, dripping banana, and twists him in his seat which pushes his right foot just ever so slightly harder on the accelerator. And accelerate they do.

And the Plaxton badge on the front of the bus is larger and clearer than any driver of a small car should have to see. He drops the fruit, jerks back his arm, spins the wheel towards the safety of his own side of the road but his foot is just ever so slightly too hard on the accelerator and the front swings in but the back swings out and round and round.

His life does not flash before his eyes – he is spared that last cliché – but his last thoughts are of the waste, the waste of his expensive private education, his three wasted years at university, the hours, years, weeks wasted with Mandy and Jojo and Bernice – the waste of someone else's time to clear him away – and as he makes one last desperate attempt, one last reflex to steer his side of the spinning car away from the parked Transit van, he skids instead into a side swipe at a tree which caves in his door, without side-impact bars, which crushes his similarly unprotected body.

He looks uninjured to Sally as she struggles free from her seatbelt, shouting at him to get out of the car while the banana continues to drip, drip, drip onto his shoes.

Shopping Basket Crown

Pieces of car and wood bark had skittered through his door yesterday, chattering over the linoleum and rattling to a halt against the stack of metal shopping baskets. The policeman had advised him to stay inside while they cordoned off the area and removed the remains of the body and the remains of the car and swept the pavement – but they had left him to pick up the shards from his floor. The red pieces weren't metal – some new-fangled fibreglass or carbon fibre or whatever it is they use now to make it cheaper to build cars and more expensive to repair them.

Today would be better. Today, only five days later than promised, the sign was coming. They had promised, even though it was Saturday, that they would be there early and the sign would be up and then, please then, there would be customers.

He had gone next door two weeks ago. His sister knew someone who knew someone who ran a company that made shop signs – but he thought he'd try to find a local firm. The shop next door had a sign that was straight and neat and spelt correctly – surely that had to be as good a recommendation as any.

"Hello." He'd knocked at the door round the back – they still had the shutters down at the front. "Sorry to trouble you."

"We're not open yet," said the dark-roots bleached-blonde.

"I know." He smiled. "I've taken over the shop next door. I'm Roy."

"Yes?" She didn't open the door any further.

"Just wanted to say hello." He paused. Her stern expression was unmoved – obviously no social niceties to be had here. "And to ask whether you can let me know who did your shop sign as I'll need one myself."

"No idea," she said. One hand slid through the hair above her ear. "Head office sorts that out. They just tell us when we're due a refresh then they send someone round. We are a national chain, you know. And, if you'll excuse me, I have a window to dress." The door closed.

The best way to get passing trade, his uncle had told him, is to have a shop full of attractive women customers. Men will be hoping for a chance encounter and women will think some of it will rub off on them – and then will hate themselves for thinking it but that will be after they've got back home with their shopping. Clearly, his attractive female customer base would have to come from elsewhere. She wasn't that good looking anyway – Roy was glad he hadn't had a chance to offer her a local-shop-worker discount.

He had found the firm in the Yellow Pages and the man had come round twenty minutes later. He'd scrawled the order on a grubby pad then taken out a business card and leaned it against the freshly painted wall while he'd scribbled out the phone number and written a mobile number next to it. The mobile phone was rarely switched on. But they were coming this morning, first thing.

Two hours later, a thin teenager was knocking on his door.

"Knock knock," he said redundantly. "Dad's just parking. You got a couple of ladders? Dad hates untying them from the top of the van."

Three quarters of an hour and one row with a parking warden later, the man knocked on his door while his son was pulling the last of the plastic cover sheet from the sign. He led Roy out into the street, under the ladder which was still propped against the door frame.

"You've put the wrong one up," said Roy.

"Nah – what you asked for," said the man. Suddenly his son was not the smiling talkative part of the operation – he was a hoodless hoodie, standing glowering sullenly next to his father. A united front, ready to deal with problem customers, argumentative types, people who did not pay on time.

"My name is Roy and this is a bakery," said Roy, calmly. "And you have put up a sign saying 'Ray's

Plaice – Breaded Fish'."

"What you asked for," repeated the man, slowly, accentuating each consonant, other than the obligatory glottal stops.

"Why," said Roy, still calmly, still a voice of reason. He cleared his throat and started again. "Why would I ask for a shop sign that's got some other bloke's name on it and a type of food I don't sell?"

"Well that would be up to you," said the man. "Here's the order I wrote down."

And he triumphantly produced a coffee-soiled crumpled sheet with 'Roy's Place – Fresh Bread' written on it.

"'Ray's Plaice – Breaded Fish'," he read, squinting at the words. He looked up. "Only I wrote 'Fish Breaded' but I knew that didn't make any sense so I swapped the words round. And I added the 'i' to make it fish-plaice not just place-place. At no extra charge for the extra letter."

"That says 'Fresh', not 'Fish'," said Roy.

"You saying my dad can't read his own writing?" said the son.

"Stay out of it, Billy," said his father.

"No, I'm not. I'm sure this is a genuine mistake. I mean, look, granted I didn't have any bread out when you were here two weeks ago but I had a bread oven, I had a price list for bread and rolls and pastries, I had pictures of bread and bakers all over the shop. And today I've got the loaves out which I baked four hours ago – you can smell them from halfway down the street. How could you have thought I'd want a sign advertising fish?"

"Then you're not saying it's a genuine mistake, are you?" said the man. "You're saying I don't know my own job. I'm telling you that I've produced, to high quality, what you asked for and have installed the same. And listen, pal. I'll be round with my brother later for payment. Cash, yeah? Discount for prompt."

The man and his son turned to go.

"Hang on a minute," said Roy, keeping it light and plaintive, stressing 'hang', not 'minute', keeping the 'we can work it out' smile on his face – but to no avail. The man turned, head angled, index finger pointing vaguely at Roy. Then he was on his way before Roy could even whisper the words 'trading standards'.

Get one little detail wrong, his uncle had told him, and the whole business can spiral out of control. Chaos theory, he had said, smiling and nodding as though he had invented the concept. Butterfly flaps its wings in somewhere foreign and over here your television aerial falls down. Roy smiled at the memory of sitting in his uncle's front room, cup of thoroughly stewed tea threatening him from the arm of the chair, listening to self-congratulatory tales of business acumen. His uncle had a point – although the problem with Ray's business was not with one little detail.

He stubbed his toe on the shopping baskets. Maybe the shopfitters were right – why did he want shopping baskets? He sold everything over the counter. He just liked shopping baskets – the noise halfway between a kerching and a clang as they slid into a stack, the pristine plastic coating over the handles which would be chipped and cracked in a matter of weeks – everything about them made him feel that he was running a proper shop. Having customers would also help with that perception.

"Cod and chips, please, mate," said the shiny-suited, fashion haircut, designer bearded man.

"Sorry, bit of a problem with the sign above the door," said Roy. "This is a bakery. Chippie's at the other end of the street. I can do you a danish or a doughnut to have after?"

"No – you're all right. Just thought I'd give the new shop a try. You want to get that sign changed – going to annoy people."

"It's quite annoying for me too," said Roy to the departing man's back.

"Excuse me?" said the man, turning around.

"Just talking to myself," said Roy.

"You want to watch that," said the man. "Sounded like you were having a go. You want to have a go? Do you?"

"Of course not," said Roy, quickly checking that, if it came to it, he could reach the bread knife first – not to use it, of course, just to move it under the counter, out of harm's way. Not only was his first customer not buying anything, he seemed to want to pick a fight as well. Today could only get better – surely.

There was some activity outside the boarded-up double-fronted shop across the street. Roy smiled – this was more like it. The recovery of the high street, the filling of the empty shops, the return of the customers, the locals who would double-park outside to pop in for an onion bagel or manoeuvre a double-buggy through his door for three rolls and a French stick – these were the people he needed, the people who sped past on their way to the out of town hypermarket – they would be reducing their food miles and buying from him. The high street recovery would float all boats, he seemed to remember some economist pundit saying on the news last week – didn't matter what the new shop was going to be, it could only be good for him.

The smart white van pulled away and Roy examined their handiwork. The navy boarding was now proudly announcing the imminent arrival of the megalith supermarket's convenience store – complete with in-store bakery.

But today could only get better, he thought. He would build his customer-base, establish loyalty, with discounts if necessary, and future-proof his business. The only alternative was to cut his losses, forfeit the deposit on the lease and give up. This was a decision he could maunder over later, once lubricated by a few drinks, while catching up on the soaps.

His uncle had never watched soap operas — which might have explained why his bakery had come crashing down after thirty-seven years of hard work — he hadn't kept up, he hadn't been watching where the country was going, he was getting up at three in the morning and tucked up in bed by seven and he saw the inside of his shop and the inside of his oven and, towards the end, too much of the inside of his till — not covered by any money. When the kids came in and started throwing things around and laughing at him he had no idea what he was supposed to do about it. He didn't know the parents and the kids didn't care what he said and he couldn't give them a clip round the ear — too many ears, and they'd probably smack him around first, and then he'd end up being the one picked up by the police. So he gave the landlord notice and retired with a small uncomfortable pension and sat in his house wondering what on earth he was supposed to do with himself now.

Roy used his inheritance to set up the shop and to repeat all of his uncle's mistakes. He smiled to himself — of course he brought the mistakes up to date and added a few new ones, just for himself, as Larkin would have had it.

A double-buggy, mucus-encrusted child on one side, shopping bag on the other, bumped and scuffed its way into the shop, clipping the stack of baskets, the mother entering some time later, on the phone, impervious to her surroundings.

"...and I don't even know why he's got the things there – who ever needed a basket in a fish shop, lucky Jake's with his granny, would have hit his foot on it..."

She looked up at Roy without pausing to draw breath, her face fell into a look of disappointment and she immediately began the tortuous process of leaving.

"...lovely smell of bread but we bake our own... yeah, I thought I could get Oliver some chips but it's not a chippie... no, I dunno why the sign..."

"You could always get him a doughnut," Roy called helpfully.

"What, and fill him with sugar?" she replied, lip twisted half in smile, half in contempt before returning to her other conversation, "No, darling, wasn't talking to you, this fishmonger baker person trying to flog me a sugar-high for Oliver, like I need a repeat of yesterday..."

Oliver was now out of the shop, along with his bag travelling companion. One sentence later, his mother followed, her conversation dribbling away down the street, "...no more than one day after the due date... Yes, why should you wait? You've got plans for the summer..."

In many ways, the shopping baskets were the fault of Mr Davies. Roy remembered the kindly old shopkeeper from his blurred childhood idyll – somewhere between the b-movie mentor who teaches the kid the value of love and hard work and the cartoon's friendly old duffer soon to be unveiled as the bad guy. Davies Groceries had been an ordinary suburban corner shop – tins and boxes and bottles and packets stacked around all four walls and the central shelving, a narrow path prone to food avalanches leading around the blind corners, convex mirrors adorning strategic points around the ceiling and, by the door, the till with its plastic price flags jumping out of their slots at the forceful press of the heavy levers, a full-blooded ding accompanying every opening of the drawer. It was vast then and so much smaller now, Mr Davies long gone but the layout, the style, the extreme use of space outliving him.

Roy and his friend Paul would joust in the shop – all shopping basket helmets, wrapping paper cardboard tube swords and kitchen paper cardboard tube daggers. A few tins would crash to the floor, once a glass jar shattered, but nothing seemed to faze Mr Davies – he enjoyed the company. Roy smiled – of course now he would be investigated for enjoying the company of two eight-year-old boys. Back then, it was their playground, watched over by kindly old Mr Davies, never unveiled as a bad guy, still remembered warmly. Roy didn't remember Paul very well though – last news was fifteen years ago when a friend of a friend told him that Paul had moved to Kansas City but couldn't remember why. Roy had lost touch with him at eleven – Roy to the grammar school, Paul to the comprehensive – no fraternising with the enemy.

He picked up one of his shopping baskets, turned it over, placed it gingerly over his head but the balance point was all wrong – it worked much better as a hat or a crown, he couldn't get the handles to lock behind his head to use it as a helmet. Another part of childhood which had to be left behind, thought Roy, as he carefully slid the basket back into the stack.

"Whatcha doing?"

He turned to face a sneer in a hood, hands in pockets, jeans low slung around hips. He tried to suppress his first instinct – feral youth, get back behind the counter, any barrier would do.

"Just reliving my youth," he said, smiling, walking back around the counter slowly, calmly. "Can I help you?"

"Yeah – what's fresh?"

"Everything," said Roy expansively, "I baked it all this morning."

"Yeah, but what you got ready to go with the chips?"

Roy's spirits sank as he prepared himself for another lost sale. He turned to look above his head, to check that the price list for the breads and the rolls and the pastries and the cakes was indeed still there and hadn't been replaced by prices for cod and haddock and plaice and saveloys and, in an instant, the bread knife was in the child's hand.

"And last night's takings – they ready to go with the chips?"

"Oh do me a favour," said Roy, sighing. "This is a bakery, I've got almost nothing in the till and I wasn't open last night. I don't sell fish and I don't sell chips and I don't want a fight and there's nothing here worth stealing so why don't you just take a doughnut and we'll forget this ever happened."

"Whah?"

Roy leaned in close. "Do you smell fish and chips? Do you see salt and vinegar and pickles and gherkins? This is a bakery – I just need to change the sign above the door."

"Whatever – give me what's in the till and a doughnut then." The smirk widened and deepened. "Friday night – busiest night, isn't it? Fish on Fridays and all that claptrap. Give us the money and then," he spat on the floor, "then we'll forget this ever happened."

Roy looked out of the window. Cars and buses trundled past. A man in a fluorescent jacket was picking up litter on the other side of the street, an ambulance screeched and wailed its way around the sleepy traffic, five men in football boots jogged past towards the park – it was a normal weekend for everyone else, probably a normal weekend for the kid in front of him trying to empty out his already nearly empty till. Today had to get better, starting right now.

He opened the till.

"I know you people hide the big cash in the bottom of the drawer, under that tray thing."

Oh, so I'm one of 'you people' now, am I, thought Roy. Part of the wide international brotherhood of robbed shopkeepers.

"Whaddya take me for?" continued the boy.

"There's no money there either," said Roy, lifting up the tray. "Only this fifteen quid in change. Now why don't you just take it and go away?"

"Let's have a look at your watch and phone," said the robber, warming to his theme. He thrust the bread knife vaguely in Roy's direction. "Unless you've got other plans for the morning."

"Okay, okay, that's enough," said Roy. He sighed. "Just let me tell you something about me and, once I've finished, if you still want them, you can take the fifteen quid, my cheap watch and knackered old mobile."

The youth glanced towards the door and, once satisfied that there wasn't a queue forming behind him, twisted his mouth into an approximation of a threatening smile.

"All right," he said. "Just make it short and, er, punchy."

"On the day I was born," said Roy.

"I really don't think we've got time to go that far back."

"On the day I was born," repeated Roy sternly, "my grandmother looked out of her window and

saw ten magpies in her back garden. She was
superstitious, bless her, and she turned to my
grandfather and said something like, 'It's either
going to be a golden boy or a bastard girl' – I'm
paraphrasing, as I don't think she used words like
'bastard' much."

"What are you talking about?"

"Don't you know the rhyme about magpies? One
for sorrow, two for joy, three for a girl, four for a
boy, five for silver, six for gold, seven for a secret
never to be told?"

"Nope."

"Okay, whatever. So she worked out that ten had
to be seven and three or six and four and assumed
that the secret never to be told would be that my
mum had had an affair and the girl wasn't my
father's daughter. Fortunately for her, I turned out
to be a boy so mum didn't have her mother-in-law
breathing down her neck or saying that the child
didn't look much like its dad. Unfortunately for me,
I had to put up with her saying that I was a golden
child, going to be showered with gold, going to
have enough gold for everyone, that it was only a
matter of time."

"So you're telling me it hasn't happened yet?"

"Take a look at the place. I had to close early
yesterday because someone crashed his car into that
tree and this stretch of pavement was closed. And I
spent an hour picking bits of car and tree out of the
floor. Then this morning some idiot put the wrong

sign over the door and tried to tell me it's my fault. On top of that, a supermarket with an in-store bakery is about to open across the street. I've only had two customers all day, if you can call them that as they didn't buy anything and just gave me abuse. And now I've got you in here. So what I'm saying is – give me a break."

"You're breaking my heart."

"All right, take the fifteen quid but leave me alone."

"You, my friend, have a deal," said the youth, smiling. "No hard feelings."

The man in the shiny suit had quietly walked back into the shop. Roy would have expected leather, not rubber, soles on the man's shoes but he seemed to be able to walk silently across the tile-effect lino. He smiled as he caught Roy's eye and put his finger to his lips.

"Okay," said Roy slowly. He opened the till and with fingers too enured to failure even to tremble with fear or disappointment, he pulled the two bank notes from under their spring-clips. "Oh, leave us the fiver," he said, "I need to pick up some dinner on the way home."

The youth thrust the bread knife closer to Roy, two fingers extended to snatch the notes, the other hand having not moved from the trouser pocket all the time he'd been in the shop.

"You're all heart, you are," said Roy, as he leaned forward to put the notes into the outstretched fingers, and as the youth didn't have time to spin around when he heard the ching of the basket being pulled from the stack but instead he fell forwards into the counter as the basket caught him hard against the side of his head, and as the criss-cross metalwork made criss-cross lacerations across his cheek and forehead and ear and broke his nose and cracked three of his molars and sent him jerking forwards, only forwards, so that his arm flailed and his fingers missed the money but the blade found Roy.

The man in the shiny suit dropped the basket at the sight of Roy, all frothing at the mouth and juddering spasms as the freshly baked bread and rolls and fancies were glazed crimson. He gagged but managed to retain his cod and chips while the basket fell, neatly, as a crown over the head of the robber lying motionless on the floor, handles hinging out around the ears. He ran towards the door, then paused, then returned to slide the fifteen pounds out from under Roy's fluttering fingers.

Ukulele Cradle King

He swung his legs over the side of the bed – the sooner the day started, the sooner he could stop worrying about his life and lose himself in the routine. Even his three-year-old niece knew – uncle Russell, do minutes take longer if you're not doing anything? How do you answer that? He'd settled for a glum yes and hoped that there wasn't a supplementary question coming.

Last night, Russell Stevens had again refuted the theory that dying in a dream will lead to death in real life. A ridiculous idea, Russell had always thought – after all, if someone dies in their sleep, who would ever know what their final dream had been about? And how would anyone know that any dreams had ever been about death if it hadn't been for all the people who had woken up and blabbed about them? He hadn't blabbed about it – he'd always thought that there was little more tedious than people telling you about their dreams like it was supposed to signify something interesting. All dreams signified the same thing – a free-wheeling brain coughing up the experiences of the past few days, chewing them over and then swallowing them back down. Dreaming of falling, dreaming of lying paralysed in a war-zone, dreaming of running through a cornfield – most of them could be tracked directly to some late night action film which his subconscious had clearly been following too closely.

He had been staring through the window for about five minutes. He surreptitiously glanced at his watch – not even half past nine. He barely suppressed a groan although a yawn surprised him and sneaked through. It was going to be another very long day, he thought – these minutes were going to take a long, long time even though he was doing something.

The hunger pangs didn't help. He would usually have grabbed a pasty on the way to work but, this morning, he hadn't taken his usual route because his sister-in-law had told him about a new bakery that had just opened on the high street. She'd gone on about it for so long that he thought today he'd try it, hoping that he'd hate the food and could make her feel bad enough that she'd stop nagging him – and then he could go back to his usual. Instead he was going to make her feel bad about the fact that the place didn't seem to exist. Just across from where the supermarket is about to open, she'd said. No sign above the door but you can smell the fresh bread from the other end of the street, she'd said. All he found across the street from the supermarket hoarding was a closed-down fish and chip shop and a hairdresser. There was a small sign in the window of the chippie saying that it would soon become a children's clothes shop – which was all very well for children who wanted clothes but didn't help the fact that he didn't have time to go anywhere else to get his breakfast.

He picked up his cardboard coffee cup. It seemed very light – he must have finished it – and, right on cue, his bladder started grumbling and burning. His boss had been lecturing him about taking too many comfort breaks, as he put it, and the other two alternatives didn't bear thinking about. He just had to focus on something that would distract him, preferably something that wasn't to do with liquids. He shifted his feet and nudged the ukulele. It lay resplendent in its cardboard box, the accoutrement of a down-at-heel mobster for whom a proper instrument case to conceal his tommy gun was still out of reach. He was lucky the security services hadn't set the alert at 'heightened' this morning or he might have found himself in the back of a police van before he had a chance to tell them he couldn't even play the thing and that, even if he could, it was missing its E string.

You work near the shop. His brother had phrased it like a statement, spoken it like an instruction, handed the thing to him as he was leaving and slipped a twenty into his pocket. Get them to restring it, would you. Keep the change.

Shouldn't be any more than that.

Don't hurry to get it back, said his sister-in-law. She'd said it all light and frothy but there was a hardness in the sentence somewhere, a hardness that had set in after countless evenings of twanging out the same three chords over and over and over again and over telephone conversations and over television programmes and over unwanted guests.

Only if you're able to get as far as the shop, his brother had added. He'd made the mistake of talking about the dream, about lying unable to move, about the dream-fear and the waking-sweat and all of a sudden his brother had seized his conversation, his story, his damaged psyche and started talking about some ancient Greek paradox.

Well excuse me, Aristotle, his sister-in-law had said.

It wasn't Aristotle – it was Zeno, corrected his brother. Zeno, in what many considered a mathematical joke, had proved that it was impossible to move, impossible to ever get anywhere whether you're in a nightmare or on a suburban street.

Just think about getting to the postbox at the end of the street, his brother had said. Sixteen houses – shouldn't take long. But first you've got to pass eight houses to get half-way there. Then four houses to get half-way through what's left. Then two, then one, then half, then a quarter, then an eighth, then a sixteenth of a house and so on for ever and ever and ever. And there are an infinite number of places to get past before you reach the postbox and you're never going to have time to visit an infinite number of places so you'll never get there.

And that, he concluded with an after-dinner speaker's flourish, was the excuse I gave for not sending back last year's tax return – it was impossible for me to post it. They still fined me, though. Philistines.

He paused to give Russell a chance to laugh or smile or raise his eyebrows or show any sign of appreciation of his wit – none came – before he continued. So only take the uke to the shop if it's actually possible for you to get there.

Well excuse me, Zeno, his sister-in-law had said.

Suddenly he realised that something concerning him had just happened in the meeting and that everyone in the room was staring at him. He smiled and nodded but knew that wouldn't be enough. Clearing his throat, he reached for the control box.

As the cradle slowly descended, he gave a parting wave to the men in the boardroom. He dipped his squeegee into the bucket and prepared to start cleaning the windows by the secretaries. He remembered the old days when the windows could be opened and when the nice-looking secretary used to get him a cup of tea and a biscuit. Now all they could do was smile – but none of them did. They just pretended he wasn't there. Mind you, a cup of

tea was the last thing he needed right now –
although, if the window still opened, he could
climb in to use their loos without his boss knowing
about it. And the toilets on fourteenth always used
to be quite swish – much better than the ones for
service personnel in the basement, which always
had that strong smell of a disinfectant well past its
sell-by date.

A window-cleaner with a ukulele – how
hilarious.   He was sure his brother could have
dropped the blasted thing off himself but he was just
so tickled, so absolutely insufferably smug at his
masterful wit, that he simply had to have it enacted.
And the damnable thing was too big to fit in his
locker so it lay beside his buckets on the floor of the
cradle, the cardboard slightly spattered by the soapy
water, the instrument perilously close to having a
foot put through it. At that height, you do not, you
do not, you DO NOT look down, even to dip into
the bucket, even to scratch your ankle, even to push
the buttons to wind up or wind down or scuttle
across. You simply know where everything lies,
you have a place for it all and your hands can find
everything you need while you project yourself into
the room to ignore the height, to ignore the cold, to
ignore the blustering wind. The last thing you need
is a ukulele lying where you would normally step to
clean the glass over by that edge of the frame.

A gust of wind caught his hair and swung the
cradle slightly. It didn't bother him – he'd been up

in his office, as he called it, in worse conditions than this. He'd gone up when he only had to hold his arm straight out to clean the windows – the wind swung him around enough to wipe backwards and forwards across the glass.

It had been a windy day all those years ago, the day when he hadn't held out his arm and Becca hadn't either and Bobby had seen something, they'd never know what, he'd never had a chance to tell them, and he'd stepped sideways and between the cars, parked just far enough apart (heaven knows how the Peugeot driver was supposed to get out) for him to get through and into the street. And the squealing of the barely legal tyres had cut through the whoosh and wuther of the wind and he'd never made a sound apart from the falling and crumpling onto the tarmac which sounded like nothing important, like a wet towel falling from a badly shaped hook on the back of a bathroom door, like a few telephone directories falling and landing on their open sides, the pages splaying out from the impact; not like a shattering, a keening, an absolute destruction, a ruination, a tearing apart from Becca, from his home, from his job, from his friends and into the realm of someone who must be bucked up, someone who must be helped and cheered and given little jobs and big smiles and full support until he suffocated under it all. But up here, even with this week's task of the ukulele to restring, he had the fresh air, he had the solitude, he didn't have anyone's pity or sympathy. They either ignored him or they glared as though they resented his being there, spying on them as they picked their noses and adjusted their underwear and played solitaire and wrote their emails – as though they thought the windows should be cleaned in the evenings or the weekends or by a machine.

One of the secretaries looked up and jumped at the sight of him, literally jumped, the gas piston suspension of the chair gently bobbing back to calm. She had to be new because she smiled, tipped her head to one side, fanned her hands out, miming the silly-me persona. He waved back, sending a few dribbles from the window scraper running down and across the glass, tracing out swirling patterns with the rise and fall of the wind. The high buildings funnelled the wind around them – tightened, exaggerated, shepherded it, sometimes the slightest change in wind direction leading to a switchback as the air found it easier to come round the other side of the monolith, and it blew and blew, now from the left, now from the right while, way down, at ground level, where he could never look, the trees were as calm as the skirts of the smokers standing around the doorways, a slight rustle, a tender and gentle flap, nothing more.

She made eye contact again. She yawned and stretched, looked at her watch, grimaced, turned back to her screen, looked back around at him, smiled. Before he could stop himself, he held up a wait-a-moment finger, reached down, opened the box and stood before her, a ukulele king in his window cleaner's cradle, mouth set in a Formby gurn, nails striking up and down against the strings, fingers pressed randomly against the fretboard. She laughed, and she shook while she laughed, and he heard her through the triple glazing and heads nearby turned to look at her and he quickly put the instrument back in its box and started cleaning the glass again, face impassive, nothing to do with him, but a quick wink for her when she glanced over to him again.

Could it be time for him to move on, for him to meet someone else, to start again, to hope for better, to settle down? A first meeting through soundproof glass was not auspicious. She looked up, he mimed having a drink, she smiled, shrugged, looked down, looked up, nodded, pointed to her watch, held up ten fingers and then two. He pointed down, all the way down, she nodded then, eyebrows raised, she picked up a sheet of paper and wrote in large capitals 'lobby at noon'. She held up the paper. He smiled and nodded. She had no ring – he was getting ahead of himself.

Becca hadn't worn a ring. Perhaps she would have fallen for the first window cleaner who came along. Perhaps she wouldn't – it wasn't any of his business any more. After his compassionate leave had turned into sick leave and then into a no hard feelings voluntary redundancy, she had quickly moved out. Since eight months before he had been born, Bobby had been the only thing keeping them together and, without him, there was nothing to hide behind, no shade for either of them from the searchlight glare of the other, no shade for her from the desperate entreaties in his eyes asking for – what? Forgiveness? Pity? Love? And no shade for him from her blinding contempt for the weak man who could not move on, who would not accept that the end of one life could not mean the crumbling of another two. Get a job, she had insisted but, when she discovered that the once soon-to-be high-flying architect was now flying high washing down the buildings he should have been designing, she had moved out and away and her old phone number no longer worked and her parents wouldn't give him her new address and they either threw away his letters or she did. She could not look into her grief and so kept on moving and he was just a reminder that they never worked out who was to blame and as long as he wasn't in the room she could carry on telling herself it was him.

He told himself it was him too. Some nights he dreamt that he went to the park with Bobby and he passed four girls who were carrying beautiful flowers which they had pilfered from the park. He told Bobby to stand still and went and told the girls that the park was for everyone and that the flowers weren't for them to take away and that they should come back and plant some bulbs to replace the flowers and the girls shouted for their father and a brute of a man suddenly appeared and grabbed him, then shoved him, then punched him and he fell to the ground and heard Bobby crying but he blacked out and when he came round in his dream, Bobby was gone. And he ran around the park looking for his son or the brute or the four girls but there was no one there but there were so many flowers, the colours over-saturated and exaggerated as though Technicolor was still new and showing off its gaudy dress, so many flowers that he could have just let the girls steal their handfuls and it wouldn't have really mattered and then Bobby would still have been next to him, ready to run to the playground. And then he woke up, certain that Bobby was only missing in the park and the worry was then swallowed by the resurgent grief and he cried all over again as though for the first time.

He scuttled the cradle across the glass, the crane three floors above him sliding and clattering along its track. He was back in familiar territory – no one looked up, the man looking out of the window carried on looking out of the window, not a flicker in his eye to show that he acknowledged the presence of another human, a hard-working man improving his view. The man leaned against the desk partition, his body language hinting at a chat-up line, the posture of his target suggesting that he didn't have a hope.

The ukulele had surprised him.

Maybe it would have been different with the fourth string but the sound was richer than he had expected from the scratchy old records and juddering old films. And the three notes he had happened upon had created something he would never have expected – harmony. He was itching to try it again. He turned away from the glass, crouched down into the cradle so he could not see across or back or down. He opened the box and admired the varnished mass-produced wooden body, the nylon strings ending at the four white pegs, one sadly bereft of purpose. I'll get you fixed up, he found himself saying to the instrument. The white rings around the hole in the middle looked cheaply printed and the bronze-effect frets were losing their sheen but the ukulele looked like, he searched for the word, it looked like fun. And he sure as hell hadn't let much fun into his life for a while.

His brother had stuck a home-made chord-fingering chart on the inside of the box. There were only seven chords listed, showing that he was more than a three-chord man, but not much more. Without the fourth string, F major became minor and plaintive, C major became hollow but G major was a revelation as three happy strings sang out with pleasure each time Russell ran his rough thumb over them. There was too much twang and unevenness but even an amateur like him could not stifle the warmth, the chirpiness, the sheer uncaring joy of the instrument – still the proper soundtrack for window-cleaning even after all these years.

A date for coffee and maybe lunch and now a new hobby – Russell's morning seemed to have recovered from its hungry and sleep-deprived beginnings. He gently put the ukulele back into its box and, turning as he stood, finished cleaning the window pane. He was relieved to see that he had not caused a crowd to gather on the other side of the glass – perhaps unsurprisingly since none of them had given any indication of having noticed him in the first place.

The distractions of ukulele playing and secretarial flirting appeared to have appeased his bladder – he hadn't had any complaints from it for a while although, as he realised it was nearly his break time, the urgency began to throb again. He reached for the control box to winch himself back up.

Up and over the secretarial floor, past the boardroom where the same faces were still staring at the same slide on the same screen with the same expressions and up past the service level towards the roof dock, at which point the left cable slipped on its bearings, snagged itself between the cog and the mount and the roof edge and the balustrade and, with a deeply unsatisfying ping and a slight ricochet like the sound he used to get from his Slinky toy which he had never had a chance to give to Bobby, the left cable broke like his brother's ukulele string.

The cradle swung from horizontal to vertical and then past vertical as it fully emptied itself of its cargo. The ukulele spiralled down like a fattened sycamore seed. The bucket chased after its sprinkling contents. Russell silently fell towards the earth.

No one looked up as he passed the boardroom and the secretaries must have all been busy as he didn't even have a chance to cancel his coffee date as he fell.

It takes such a long time in the lift, thought Russell. The lift stops at every floor as people get in, travel up or down a floor or two, talk to one another or, more usually, don't, and stare at the doors or their feet instead. No one ever spoke to him or even appeared to notice him. This way is much faster, he thought, but it's a hard trick to repeat.

He wasn't sure why he was so calm. He felt as though he were flying next to his body as it plummeted to the ground – he felt disconnected from what was certain to happen next. He saw people walking on the pavement and hoped he wasn't going to land on one of them. He wondered if he should be shouting or screaming – at least it would get them to move out of the way – but he couldn't bring himself to make any sound at all.

He passed the fifth floor where he thought the man sitting at the table by the window, enjoying a mug of coffee and Danish pastry, might have noticed him – but he shot past too quickly to be sure.

There was a dirty stripe across the building at the fourth floor. The people who worked there had refused to pay for their windows to be cleaned. Russell used to clean their windows anyway – he didn't want his building to look dirty. Whenever his boss complained, Russell used to say that it must have rained so hard that those windows just looked clean. His boss had been kind enough not to point out that the windows he had actually cleaned didn't look much better than those that had apparently only been rained on.

The gym was on the third floor. He couldn't bear to be looking in during the lunch hour, watching all those people sweating and straining and gasping on various machines. It all looked like torture to him. Russell had always hated gym when he had been at school and didn't see why he should change his mind now.

The second floor had frosted glass all the way around. He'd always meant to find out what was going on in there. One of his colleagues thought it must be medical experimentation but then he did watch too many late night conspiracy theory movies.

There was no first floor on this side of the building because the reception was double-height. Always took longer to clean, he thought wistfully, since there wasn't a floor and a ceiling to break it up. Not something for him to worry about any more though, he thought.

Only one double-height window to go. Thoughts of Zeno filled Russell's mind. I will never hit the ground, he thought. First I must get half-way down this glass, then half of what is left, which is a quarter, then an eighth, then a sixteenth, then a thirty-second. It will go on forever – there are an infinite number of places to go to on the way down, I'll never reach the bottom, I can never be smashed to oblivion on the pavement.

I must hold on to this, I must think faster, there is so much for my brain to do, it must work harder to get it all done. Then every part of my journey downwards, even though half the length of the previous part, will feel like it takes the same amount of time. The more I am thinking, the faster my thoughts can run, the harder my brain can work, the more I can pack in, the longer the descent will be.

I was wrong to tell my niece that minutes take longer if you're not doing anything. If I can make my brain run faster, time and gravity will back away and the blink of an eye needed to fall the next couple of centimetres will be time enough for me to have my whole life not flash before my eyes but be played out in a calm and orderly fashion.

And the half of one blink needed to fall the centimetre after that will be time enough to consider and re-evaluate the whole of my life and to accept that the death of Bobby was just a freak accident and that he should be mourned but he should not be a haunting presence destroying the rest of the lives of those who loved him.

And the quarter of one blink needed to fall the next half centimetre will let me play out the rest of my life, making a new start with the secretary (even though I don't yet know her name), from a coffee date to settling down together and raising a family and watching the children grow into adults and leave home and start families of their own. I will master at least eight chords on the three-string ukulele. I will see the grandchildren to dote over as we are willingly press-ganged into babysitting and as we spoil them with chocolate and gifts and wonder why they don't visit when they become teenagers and we gradually decay together through our old age.

And the eighth of one blink needed to fall the next quarter centimetre will let me refine and improve the way the rest of my life will go, redress the balance of joy to heartache, right through to the final rush to hospital and the adoring children and adoring grandchildren in concentric circles around my bedside, being chivvied by the nurse for exceeding the maximum number of visitors as I slowly slip blissfully away to the gentle beep and gasp of hospital machinery.

And my brain will have had a full lifetime during its descent and will be old and weary while still floating towards the ground and will expire before

its destruction.   And when it has shut down
peacefully, time will regain its grip and my body
will meet its grisly fate but I will truly have died
during the fall, not from the impact. And I'll never
be able to blab about it.

Footnote: A blink takes about one third of a
second. Terminal velocity for a man in freefall is
about 120mph or 55 metres per second. At this
speed, a man would fall about 2cm in the blink of
an eye.

No Second Swing

Boom tumble thump crash crack and silence. Until then, everything had been going so well for Colin. However, that was the point when things began to really look up for his book.

In the financial turmoil, when the banks discovered that the phantom slippery money they had been throwing around didn't actually exist at all; when companies large and small realised that they hadn't read the small print carefully enough and that there was in fact no reason why the bank couldn't call in the loan and cancel their credit; when employees of every age, colour, creed and orientation, with dependants or no dependants, with tight but manageable mortgages or a modest rent to find each month, suddenly found themselves without a job, without the wherewithal and without a hope of holding onto their homes, their cars, their self-respect – Colin's employer went bankrupt and he lost his job.

Colin wasn't bothered. Most of his income had been carefully parcelled away into high interest savings accounts for years – he had never trusted the casino of the stock market and his money was intact. And so he could tell himself, frequently, that he wasn't bothered, that he was free, that it was his time, that finally he could write that novel. Every day he set his target and he sat and he wrote and he rewrote. Some days he went sailing past his target number of words, on a roll, the sentences flowing out faster than his fingers could type them. Most days the hours went by on Wikipedia and The Onion as he filled his head with culture and facts, some well researched, some invented by vested interests, all fascinating, all easier than nursing the story along.

His expenses were minimal, he wore sweaters in the winter and kept his thermostat frugally low. He went to the cheaper supermarket and he learnt the times when the guy with the handheld barcode scanner and label printer went around marking down the older goods. He feasted on cut-price, just in date, groceries. He drank mainly tap water. His friends phoned him, he let them pay for the calls until they wondered why he never phoned them and the intervals between the friendly but unsatisfying chats grew ever longer.

The book swelled. The story developed. He went back, retrofitting facts and misdirection to service plot twists only just invented. He changed characters' names on whims, letting the word processor do the work, smiling and nodding when it was done – yes, that was why he couldn't get a handle on the protagonist – her name was wrong.

He walked for exercise and to clear his head and to visit the shops where he kept up human contact with a nod and a smile for the man at the checkout, yes he had his own bag, no he didn't have the loyalty card, thank you for the voucher, have a nice afternoon, goodbye.

Some nights he cried without entirely understanding why. His life was good, he told himself. He had everything he wanted, he tried telling himself before correcting himself and pointing out that he only had everything he needed. That should be enough, he told himself. He channelled the non-specific despair into his work, threading it through the characters as they played out their pathetic, unfulfilled lives. He bubbled it away as the excitement of the story seized his cast from their terraced houses and estate cars, and developed their understanding of themselves, and taught them, and gave them something to tell their grandchildren, before leaving them satisfied with a wry smile on their faces and a glow in their chests.

One day it was finished. The sun came out, he took off one of his sweaters and moved his chair nearer to the window, leaned forward, felt the sun on his back as the printer chuntered and grumbled and shuttled to and fro, and the paper slid out until it was too high for the tray and cascaded down onto the carpet. He picked up his work, he felt the heft of it, he rubbed his hand over his stubbled chin and smiled.

Now what? Publishers hadn't been beating a path to his door only because they hadn't known about his writing – how could they have done? He looked over the spines of his books, pulled out four of his favourites, three shared a publishing house, the address was on the website, he wrote 'Submissions Department' above it, wrote a short letter introducing his book, introducing himself, encouraging them to read and to read on. He punched a hole through the top corners and strung his pages together with a red tag and slid the bundle into the envelope. Four stamps should cover it, he thought. He peeled them and stuck them and walked to the postbox on the corner and bought himself a bottle of wine on the way home.

He drank two glasses with his vegetable stir-fry dinner and put the rest in the fridge to add to the food over the coming week.

Colin emailed two of his friends, asked how they were, asked after the children, asked if they could meet him one afternoon, any afternoon, for lunch – he could come to where they worked – or for a drink one evening. Neither replied. Colin assumed the corporate spam filter was misdirecting his message, or that they no longer worked there, or that they were on holiday.

He went to the cinema in the afternoons when it was cheaper and when he could sit where he liked and when he often had the room to himself, or only had to share it with a handful of others who spaced themselves out around the cinema, possibly due to each objecting to the scent of the others. Some of the scents were potent. Colin couldn't always remember whether he had bothered to shower that morning.

The cinema was too crowded in half-term week. He started borrowing films from the library in addition to taking ten books at a time. On very cold days, he would read the books in the library to give his central heating a rest. He learned to wrap sandwiches in kitchen paper instead of foil so that he could surreptitiously eat his lunch while he was there, so that he could save a full eight hours of extra gas bill. He looked into claiming benefits but was deterred by the forms, by the security guards at the job centre, by the thought of the interviews, by the realisation that he wasn't ready to take a job, to give up on the dream, not yet, not when it couldn't be much longer before they wrote to him, apologising for the delay, congratulating him on his work, arranging a lunch meeting, producing the contract.

When four weeks had gone by, he wrote to the publishing company to ask them how they were getting on with his book. Five weeks after that, he telephoned them. Apparently they were not reading unsolicited manuscripts – no matter the quality, the sub-editor finally conceded. It was all on the website – and in something called The Writers'

Handbook. Apparently they could not send back
manuscripts without return postage. All unwanted
books were on a thing called a slush-pile, apparently
awaiting the summer holiday interns to sort through
them, to return those with stamps, email a standard
rejection to those with email addresses and box the
rest for recycling. He was welcome to come and
collect his work if he wanted it back. He was at a
loss for words but managed to say 'oh' and 'goodbye'
before hanging up.

Colin found that there was more to the internet
than Wikipedia and The Onion. He discovered any
number of vanity publishers, some masquerading as
literary agents, some affiliated with major
booksellers, most with surprisingly good rates of
return although, without the marketing budget and
know-how of a major publisher, together with the
muscle and the bribe to ensure an eye-level spot
near the door of the bookshop (or the supermarket –
Colin wasn't proud) and to ensure a place beside the
latest autobiography loosely ghost-written from the
incoherent ramblings of a minor celebrity, who was
going to have heard of Colin's book in order to
place an order?

Then, one Friday afternoon, the sort of warm
spring Friday afternoon when he used to come back
from the pub with his work colleagues and they
would belch the evidence of their outing discretely
into their coffee mugs, Colin found his answer. He
had been frequenting blogs, searching them for

anything to do with writing or publishing and there, before him on the screen, was a glowing critique of a website which was part writers' circle, part authors' opportunity knocks. For no charge, Colin could put his work onto this site, he could network, he could read the work of others while others read his writing, he would support other people's books and they would come in droves to support his – and once he had scaled the book chart, his work would be read by literary agents and publishers the length and breadth of the land, leading to a bidding war and untold wealth.

His book was up on the site forty-five minutes later and, ten minutes after that, he had received four messages from charming people asking him to read their books, in return for which they would read his. He put the lasagne in the microwave and the garlic bread in the oven and the salad in the bowl and, one microwave chirrup later, he settled in for the night.

Two hours later he knew that his book was far too good for the uneducated masses who had flooded the website with their tawdry little tales and yet, with the right incentive, he could get them all to support him and his book would rise, higher and higher. Success beckoned but it would need a system, it would take work and his dignity would not be intact by the end of it. No matter – Colin knew that the end would justify the means.

***

Dear Colin,

Forgive me spamming you! You probably get these all the time. But then why should I be the only person not asking you to take a look at my little book and, if you're feeling generous, to give it your support?

It's called "To Kill A Blocking Word" and it's all about the trouble I had finishing my novel. And the novel is about a writer finishing a novel. I'm hoping Charlie Kaufman will do the film adaptation!

I'm already supporting your book, of course. I love it – sorry, I can't give you any advice or pointers as I couldn't find anything to criticise at all.

Best wishes,

Trudie

***

Colin had spent two months learning the system, playing the game, being canny and self-serving while trying to appear altruistic and fair-minded. He had left lengthy critiques on others' books and supported those he felt were going to rise. He had kept a close eye on what the long-time members were up to and threw himself into the affray. A nudge here, an adjustment there – he watched the effect it had on his position and he plotted graphs and he drew conclusions. His book was finally in the top two hundred but his personal position as reader was number one. His support was now worth more than anyone else's.

And so they came to him, supporting his book

and begging for his support in return. Generally he would oblige, partly to hold onto his top spot, partly to ensure he didn't get a reputation as someone who didn't reciprocate. His book was on the move – upwards, ever upwards. He thought another three months would do it, he would have the double-first and would never again need to abase himself with semi-literate drivel.

But occasionally he hardened his stance and declared that there was a level beneath which he would not, could not stoop. "To Kill A Blocking Word" was a long, long way beneath that level – indeed, if he could anthropomorphise the book for a moment (using an analogy as bad as any in the book itself), even if it leapt up and down with its hands above its head, its fingers would not have grazed that level. Still, he wasn't brave enough to say what he actually thought.

***

Dear Trudie,

Thank you for your message and for your kind words about my book. Many thanks also for supporting it. I have added your book to my list and will get around to it shortly.

Colin

Dear Colin,

Sorry to hassle you but I just wondered whether you had started to read my book. It's been quite a few days. I hope it's grabbed your attention so much that you can't put it down! Sorry I posted such a lot of it – if you find you can't tear yourself away.

Seriously, if there's anything you don't like about it, please tell me. I want to be a better writer and any help from a wonderful author like you would be priceless.

Best wishes,
Trudie

Dear Trudie,

I'm sorry – I thought I had already read and supported your book. I must be confused. Blame it on my age! I'll get around to it in the next few days.
Colin

Dear Colin,

It's been another week. If you don't like my book at all and don't want to support it and don't have the time to write any feedback for me, that's okay! I won't bite! Just tell me how much of it you read so I know what page you were on when you got bored. I'm not trying to hassle and I've got a thick skin so just tell it to me straight.

Best,
Trudie

Dear Colin,

I know you've been active on the site because I can see all the wonderful feedback you're giving to other writers. Please don't ignore me. I don't know why I've offended you but, if you want to make up for your rudeness, you could just support my book without leaving any feedback. (I'm joking, of course – I wouldn't expect a man of your integrity to support a book he didn't like!!)

Kisses,

Trudie

Dear Colin,

I know you're playing the site because the comment you left on that cricket-bodice-ripper piece of garbage "One New Over, The Cuckold's Vest" bore no resemblance to anything that happened in the story. And you even got the name of the main character wrong. So why won't you help me? I just don't understand.

Look – how would it hurt you? If you support my book, all those sycophants who copy whatever you do would support my book too. It's not like my book would overtake yours – you're into the top hundred already.

Come on, Colin, throw this dog a bone.

Love,

Trudie

Dear Colin,

Congratulations on reaching the top seventy-five.

I am hurt and upset that you ignore me. I find your rudeness unforgivable. You're in the phone

book. See you soon.
  Big hugs,
  Trudie

  Dear Trudie,
  I'm sorry I kept missing your messages. I
stopped looking at my inbox when it got so full and
I've been unwell recently. I really wasn't
deliberately ignoring you. I will definitely take a
look at your book today or tomorrow.
  Humble apologies,
  Colin

  Colin,
  You're a bad liar and I know it was you that
reported me to the site administrators. I've got a
lovely little warning from them about how stalking
is against the terms and conditions of the site. I've
copied their warning, together with the truth about
what's happened and the truth about you – and I've
put them all on my 'all about me' page. All publicity
is good publicity and, if it scares a few more people
into supporting my book, then all the better!
  I'm busy this afternoon but I'll probably be
popping round some time next week. Postman
seems to be able to get into your block of flats with
the 'tradesmen' button as long he's there in the
morning.
  Love ya,
  Trudie

***

Elbows on desk, fingers twisting the hair above his temples, Colin stared at the computer screen. Maybe Trudie was crazy or maybe she was winding him up for her own amusement. He considered for a while and then started writing. He gave it to her straight and told her that he hadn't liked her book from the moment he saw the title. Reading the first paragraph had been like wading through treacle, the words sticking and clogging as he desperately thrashed his way to the end of the sentence. By the end of the first paragraph he was exhausted. At the end of the first page he had to close his eyes and settle his breathing. It was neither funny nor moving nor profound nor quotidien, he could not imagine it appealing to anyone anywhere. He had abandoned the first chapter part-read, bypassed the second chapter, assuming it untrustworthy owing to its proximity to the first, and resumed with the excruciatingly awful chapter three. The protagonist may well have suffered writer's block, as may the protagonist's book's protagonist – but that was nothing compared to the reader's block he had experienced. He was reminded of Dorothy Parker's comment, although he had forgotten the book to which she was referring when she had said, "This is not a novel to be tossed aside lightly. It should be thrown with great force".

He breathed out and sent the message on its way. He was being harsh but fair. Trudie needed to know that she was not an author, that she could never be an author and that she should move on, should find another career and a hobby (other than writing) as a creative outlet. The relief shuddered through him, he smiled, the situation was defused, he could move on. He celebrated by showering and washing his hair. Unless she was truly deranged, she would thank him for his time, maybe send a barbed rebuttal of his criticism and trawl the site looking for someone else to attempt to bully.

The firm triple knock on the door caught him by surprise. No one had visited in weeks, or perhaps it was months. Friends would use the entryphone on the pavement. He was not on speaking terms with anyone in the downstairs flats – he had the whole of the top floor and also the final staircase (boxed in at his expense to move his front door downwards, to have the picture hanging space above the bannister, to have places to leave his shoes, formal at the top, mud-spattered wellingtons at the bottom). He had considered a secondary entryphone system on his door to save the running down the stairs to open it and the running up the stairs with the guests, but there were no guests and he only went downstairs to go out and then walked slowly upstairs when he came home and straightened the pictures and lined up the shoes on the alternate stairs and sometimes picked mud-flecks out of the cheap carpet, unchanged since the days when the stairs had been open to all, and still carrying a little builders' dust and plaster that, on brighter days, sprang out of the floor and hung in the shafts of sunlight coming through the window.

Dum dum de dum dum. Dum dum. The second flurry of knocking preceded the snick as the card slid through the letterbox. Colin ran down the stairs and picked up the postman's card. He opened the door, put the lock on the latch, ran around the landing and called to the postman just as he was making his way out onto the street.

"Hello? Do you have a parcel for me?"

The postman turned, smiled, opened his bag and produced a fat envelope, probably not too fat for the letterbox, an envelope he recognised, although the original address had been crudely crossed out.

"Morning, sir," said the postman. "I thought you were probably out. Still, I won't mind not carrying this around for the rest of the morning."

"Wouldn't it fit?" asked Colin, frowning. He walked down the stairs to take the envelope.

"It would have," said the postman, "and, days gone by, I would have stuck it through. But there's postage due on it and management's getting tough on us letting people off. Sorry about that – the fee's on the label here..."

"Bit steep, isn't it? It didn't cost me that much to send it."

"Ah – it's a return to sender – explains the mess they made of the address. Well, whoever sent it back didn't put any stamps on it – that'll be your original cancelled postage. And then management put on the handling charge, whatever that is. I'm doing all the handling and I don't get to keep any of it."

"Of course," said Colin, palms open, friendly smile, "I know it's nothing to do with you. But I didn't bring any money downstairs!" He gave a short, nervous laugh. "I'll just be a minute."

Up the stairs, two at a time, both flights, mind the shoes, past the photograph of the Taj Mahal, clipped from the Sunday newspaper colour magazine, looking not quite straight on the wall. He'd deal with that when he'd paid the postman, maybe get his spirit level onto it as it's tricky with stairs and the join of the wallpaper not being vertical. Coins jingling, he made his way back downstairs, paid the man, took the parcel, bade him a good day and back upstairs, all the way up to his lounge to tear open his envelope.

He pulled out his manuscript. It looked pristine, uncreased, untouched, no fingermarks or coffee rings. There was no 'with compliments' slip, not even a standard rejection letter. It had been slit open to obtain his details and then crudely resealed with parcel tape, his name and address scrawled beside the scribbled-out original destination. Then it had been hurled back into the postal system. With a wry smile, Colin wondered whether it had been tossed into the post lightly or thrown with great force.

"Hello Colin."

A man was standing in his hall, just a few feet away from him. Colin got to his feet, dropped his manuscript down onto the sofa, walked towards the stranger.

"Do I know you? How did you...?"

"Sorry – the door was open downstairs. I knocked but you didn't hear me so I came up. And here I am. It's great to meet you."

Colin approached him tentatively. The man was smiling, his hand was out, ready to shake. He was well dressed, clean shaven that morning, hair neatly combed, scarf insouciantly over his shoulder. Colin was in baggy knobbly tracksuit trousers, t-shirt from a long forgotten band's 1983 tour, wet hair plastered to his scalp, three days stubble on his face.

"I'm sorry," said Colin. "I don't think we've met and I wasn't expecting anyone today. Who are you?"

"Tommy."

There was an uncomfortable pause.

"I don't know anyone called Tommy."

"See if you can work it out. My full name is Thomas Rudolph Edwards. There was another Tommy at school so the teacher thought he'd punish me by using my middle name. Worked it out yet?"

Colin found himself looking around the hall to check whether there was anything Tommy might seize to use as a weapon. He saw nothing, but nothing for himself either.

"I don't really want to have this conversation here now. There's a coffee shop around the corner – left at the end of the road, first shop on the right. I can get dressed properly and meet you there in ten minutes. Is that okay?" Colin opened his arms wide, using the generally recognised shepherding body language to try to encourage Tommy to get out, walk past the shoes and the pictures, including the slightly wonky Taj Mahal and get to the other side of the door which he could close and lock and collapse against and then, only then, could he decide what had just happened.

"This won't take long. Rudolph – what's that normally abbreviated to? Come on, Colin! A man of your intellect – this shouldn't be hard."

"Well, Rudy I suppose."

"Good man! But I'm Thomas Rudolph so Mark Jones (I had to sit next to him at school; I do wonder where he is now, which prison, or which investment bank or which graveyard) yes, Mark Jones decided I should be Tee Rudolph. Or Tee Rudy. Or... Trudie. But enough about me – what's our plan for the afternoon? I thought we could do a line-by-line critique of each other's work. I know I said I'd come round next week but someone cancelled on me. I hope you don't mind me popping round a bit sooner."

Colin's eyes flitted from side to side as he looked for inspiration, for a peace offering, for some money that he could give to Tommy so that he would just

go, for something he could hit Tommy with, for
something Tommy might pick up and hit him with.
He found nothing except the amused expression on
Tommy's face when he looked at him again.

"What do you say, Colin?"

Tommy had already looked around when he had
first crept up the stairs, making sure he didn't send
any shoes bouncing down, straightening the Taj
Mahal picture, checking the hall for anything
potentially dangerous like an umbrella, a golf club,
a letter knife. He saw nothing except Colin's laptop,
glowing away on the table in the living room,
logged onto Colin's 'all about me' page, Colin's
photograph smiling out at him. Just a few seconds
and he would have what he had come for – just a
little typing and a few mouse clicks. He had
wondered whether he could wait for Colin to get up,
maybe to go and make a cup of tea. He had
considered hiding round the corner, maybe behind
the bedroom door, before sneaking over to the
computer once the coast was clear, click click click
and make his getaway down the stairs with Colin
none the wiser. Then he thought that wouldn't be
enough fun.

Colin was not a violent man. He could not think
of any occasion when he had ever hit anybody. He
wasn't even sure that he knew how to hit someone,
where his thumb was supposed to go when he made
a fist, he'd read something about aiming for a spot a
foot behind the person to make sure the punch was

hard enough. He'd read that the first strike should be the strongest and most vicious in case there wasn't a chance to take a second swing. All he knew about fighting he had read in works of fiction where normally the good guys win, where they find the strength they need just in the nick of time.

"Okay. Tommy – should I call you Tommy? Or do you prefer Rudy?"

"Tommy is just fine."

"Okay. Tommy. I don't really have anything to say about your book – I'm not a professional editor, I just know what I like..."

"...and you know what you don't like."

"Yes! That's it! And I'm sorry that I don't like your book, but that's just my own personal opinion. I don't normally read books in that genre and..."

Tommy was listening intently, looking Colin in the eye as he spoke, a slight smile on his face – Colin was uncertain whether it was a friendly smile of forgiveness or a smirk suggesting that this little game had some distance yet to run. He inched closer while talking and, in the middle of his own sentence, sent a fist – a hesitant, reluctant fist – swinging towards Tommy's solar plexus. Tommy caught his wrist and elegantly pivoted around. Colin toppled across the hall and, his own weight working against him, tripped over Tommy's foot and found the stairs. As he went down, his face dislodged a pair of shoes, good shoes from a high step which bounced and tumbled down, knocking over others. He saw the photograph which he had been about to straighten, and wondered whether perhaps it didn't need doing. He heard the crash and the rumble that he was making, he heard the crack from somewhere in his body just before he slid to a halt.

Almost before the real-world Colin had stopped falling down the stairs, the online Colin had supported Trudie's novel 'To Kill A Blocking Word', leaving a glowing review praising its unusual narrative structure, intriguing characterisation, tight plotting, surprising twists and turns and a knock-out ending.

Tommy stepped over Colin and let himself out, making sure he took the door off the latch and closed it firmly behind himself.

In the coming weeks, Colin stopped supporting books on the website. He had built enough credit over the preceding months to hold the top reader spot for a while before being overtaken by more eager, more vital, young authors. The online Colin slowly slid down the readers' chart and fewer authors supported his book in the hope of reciprocation. But enough of them still did for the book to continue upwards, albeit at a slightly reduced speed. By the time it hit the top ten, Colin's message box had three enquiries from literary agents, keen to read the whole manuscript. When it entered the top five, he had seven agents and a few small publishing houses trying to arrange a meeting, or a lunch, or a telephone call.

Only one tried to contact him a second time. After waiting a week and getting no reply to the electronic message, an enterprising summer holiday intern discovered that he was listed in the phone book. She dialled the number but the phone just rang and rang. It wasn't worth pursuing further – there were plenty more authors desperate to be found.

Rogue Santa

"Everybody say, 'Way-Oh, Way-Oh, Way-Oh'!" His voice leapt an octave as he suddenly sang the line, arms furiously gesticulating to the audience to join in as he switched to unamplified, and unimpressive, beat-boxing.   His beard swayed menacingly.

Three more of the five-year-olds began to cry. Another two started when he attempted a Bhangra head move. His eyes moved to the left, his beard slid to the right and the bell at the end of his hat rang to its own syncopated beat.

"Do something!" hissed Mrs MacIntyre to Mr Swanson.

Mr Swanson stood up, rictus grin across his face. "Now then," he said, addressing the cross-legged brood all twinkly-eyed before flicking a cold glare at the man beside him, the man standing in his space.

"Ah," interrupted the guest, back to booming his overly fruited baritone, "Mr Swanson! Tell me, boys and girls, has Mr Swanson been a good boy this year?"

Mr Swanson's attempted joviality in delivering, "I think we've covered this already" was entirely submerged by the bellow of "No!" that attacked the stage, affecting Mr Swanson almost viscerally. He looked out to the eyes of children he no longer recognised, seeing only hatred and contempt in them, fearing that perhaps the ten-year-olds should not have read 'Lord Of The Flies' this term.

He had not thought it would come to this, indeed only twenty-four minutes earlier he had felt the traditional warm glow of well-being as the annual ritual had begun, as he saw the man arrive. He had watched him enter the room, seen the children become wide-eyed with wonder and remembered once again why, two years after he could have taken early retirement, he instead chose to spend his days here.

Twenty-four minutes earlier, ringing the school dinner bell, dressed in the school's cheap but effective supermarket polyester red suit, complete with cotton-wool cushion fat-pack, itchy elasticated beard-and-moustache combo and red hat unfortunately equipped with a jester's bell at the end of it (perhaps due to a misunderstanding between the commissioning buyer and the Chinese sweat-shop), the father of a boy in year three strode into the hall.

Mr Miller had been forced to pull out of this year's end-of-term assembly, after many years of admirable, reliable service. He had never outstayed

his welcome – get in, do the Santa shtick for two
minutes and get out again – he had never found
those instructions difficult to follow. However, this
year his company had been taken over and there
was a compulsory, off-site, team-building Christmas
function which, for a man hoping to finally receive
his promotion after so many years of being
overlooked, would have been impolitic to avoid.
He had phoned Mr Swanson and explained his
quandary and restated how much he loved his
annual performance but that this year it simply
would not be possible, but next year, well next year
he would do his utmost to step back into the suit.
Mr Swanson had understood, Mr Swanson had
thanked him for all the years he had performed in
the past, but Mr Swanson had, in thought and hand-
gesture, cursed him for pulling out at such short
notice. He had had three days to find a replacement
Santa or have the indignity of excusing himself
from the assembly in order to suit up. That could
not be allowed to happen.

Several telephone calls later, Mr Swanson had
his volunteer. He had explained the set-up, told him
that Mrs Beech would have the costume ready at the
school reception and that he could change in the
store cupboard, thanked him profusely and
considered the matter taken care of.

And his volunteer had begun well, the voice was
right, deep and warm, with an occasional jovial
chuckle in addition to the obligatory frequent ho-ho-

ho. There had been nowhere to park his sleigh, he had told the schoolchildren, the younger ones showing a mixture of wonder and fear, the older ones a combination of contempt and boredom, so he had left it on the yellow zig-zags – did they think that would be okay?

"Yes!" they had replied.

"I do hope so," he said, "unless there's a traffic warden about to be a very naughty boy. In which case, there might be a few surprises for him in his stocking come Christmas eve."

The children had laughed, the staff had looked at each other anxiously, unsure which way he was going to go with this line. Fortunately, he didn't go anywhere with it and moved onto a different tack.

"Has everyone been good?" he asked, eyes flicking left, right, to the back of the room, to the front row.

"Yes!" came the reply, slightly louder than previously, as the children warmed to the stranger and perhaps sensed the greater importance of the question.

"Wonderful," he said, "then stand up and join me in 'Head, Shoulders, Knees and Toes'. And don't forget to look at Mrs MacIntyre when you sing 'Head'!"

Mrs MacIntyre stood up. "I wonder if perhaps we should..."

"How wonderful of you to join us!" he called and began to sing, "Head, shoulders, knees and toes, sing along! Head," looking at Mrs MacIntyre, "shoulders, knees and toes, sing along". He was quite adept at the actions, even with the fat-pack making 'toes' a difficult manoeuvre. The children joined in with the singing and, to some extent, with the actions, the youngest uncertain whether to start, or moving half-heartedly, the middle group, throwing themselves into it with gusto, the oldest standing at the back staring at the unlikely sight. The staff sat in stony silence on the stage, unsure of their next move.

Slowing half-way through the song, before the section of gradually removing the facial features, he said, "Thank you for helping me with that warm-up. Let's stop it there as we have so much more to get through. Sit down, children."

Mr Swanson stood up. In an attempt to reassert his authority, he smiled at the schoolchildren and said, "Yes, thank you children, and thank you Santa. You may be seated. And I think we can give our guest a round of applause and thank him for his time."

The children began to clap, the applause starting in the middle and slowly rippling to the front and back of the hall where a section of slow hand-clapping could be seen by the eagle-eyed Mrs MacIntyre but could not be heard by the beaming Santa Claus as he held his hands up for silence and struck fear into the staff with the blood-curdling phrase, "Thank you, but I've hardly started!"

He leapt from the stage, startling the nursery class politely sitting cross-legged on the floor at the front, strode half-way along the room, produced a deck of oversized playing cards with Santa's head on the reverse, fanned them out and asked a girl in year four to choose one. She looked across to her form-teacher, who looked to the headmistress, who shrugged despondently. The girl took a card and a complex and somewhat confusing trick ensued involving a toy rabbit, oral egg production and a long ribbon of paper streaming from Mr Swanson's top pocket with the name of the chosen eight-of-spades written across it. This led to whoops of appreciation from the back, children looking from side to side in the hope that one of their friends could explain it in the middle and incomprehension from the front, most of whom could not read quickly enough to realise the significance of the paper.

With Mr Swanson struggling to contain and control the paper snake which resisted his attempts to coil it back to a manageable size, Mrs MacIntyre stood, signalled to the children to settle down with a simple palms-down, arms slowly lowered motion and, in the welcome silence, turned to the guest. She looked him in the eye, gave a slight left-right head-shake and moved in for the quiet word. Too late, she saw the twinkle in his eye.

"Everybody happy?" he shouted. Ignoring the confused silence from the floor, he continued with, "then clap your hands! If you're happy and you know it..." He seized Mrs MacIntyre's still-outstretched arms and, singing far louder than consideration for her personal space would permit, he continued the song, punctuating each line by clapping the headteacher's hands together firmly.

"You need to stop this at once!" she hissed at him, "And let go of my arms you silly man."

"You're right," he boomed. "I am a silly man." The singing from the children petered out, helped by shushing from the children at the back who, sensing conflict, wanted to make sure they could enjoy every last word.

He released Mrs MacIntyre's wrists. Rubbing her arms pointedly, she returned to her seat, whispering "Wrap it up" over her shoulder.

"A very silly man," he continued. "Why, do you know what happened to me last Christmas?"

"No," called a single voice from the back.

"I'm not surprised," continued the voice behind the beard, "as I haven't told anyone this story. I had had one or two mince pies last year, maybe more than the usual – due to everyone being so generous to dear old me."

"We can tell," called a voice from the back. It could have been the same voice.

Alternating the song with narration, he continued, "anyway, *I got stuck up the chimney*. Really. And *I began to shout*. Do you know what I shouted? I shouted that *girls and boys wouldn't get any toys if they didn't pull me out.* And that chimney wasn't clean, you know – *my beard went black and I got soot in my sack and my nose was tickly too. Yes, I got stuck up the chimney.*"

He paused and looked out over the crowd of children. Only the older ones at the back were enjoying themselves but their grins were those of children watching the aftermath of a traffic accident that was preventing them being driven to a dull provincial museum. The middle children were uncertain whether to join in the song or to listen politely to the rambling guest. The youngest children were squirming in what could have been boredom, confusion or bladder pressure.

"Aaa-choo," he bellowed.

His brow was sweaty but he felt chilly. Maybe this job was harder than he had thought it would be. Maybe he could bring it back around if he could get the children to sneeze along with him.

"Sneeze along with me!" he shouted, waving his arms in a count-down one-two-three, "Aaa-choo".

A few of them had shouted, but most were staring. He ran the back of his hand over his forehead and signalled the one-two-three to "Aaa-choo!".

Maybe half of the children were joining him. Risking a fourth sneeze to make sure he had the audience on his side, he went straight into his finale of energetic dancing and a beat-box routine.

"Way-Oh! Way-Oh! Well? Come on, sing

along children," he called. He rubbed his forehead again and found it still clammy, still cool but now additionally swaying, strangely difficult to find accurately with his hand. How difficult can it be to find my own head, he thought, as he suddenly found himself lurching, his legs not properly responding, his view moving from the roomful of children to the fluorescent strip lighting in the ceiling. He felt twinges all over and a sharp pain in his coccyx as he hit the wooden floor.

The children applauded.   Mrs MacIntyre harrumphed and tutted. Mr Swanson rose to his feet as he saw clear viscous droplets ease through the corner of the man's mouth and ooze across his cheek towards the floor.

Mrs Beech opened the side door of the hall and walked discretely towards Mrs MacIntyre. She broke her stride when she saw the red suited mound lying in the centre of the stage. "Who's that?" she whispered to the headteacher.   "I've got Mr Whitman in reception. He's really sorry to be late – a crash on the High Street closed the road. I gave him the costume because I could hear the assembly was still going on..."

Mr Swanson looked up. "Get the children out of here," he said. "This is a real beard."

Nocturnal Crème Brûlée

Where can I start? The story is complex and tangled and I have forgotten how some of the pieces join. Frankly I am as confused as anyone. I'll work through it, maybe it'll make some sense to me by the end.

Sandy lived here for a while. Imagine that! A girl called Sandy, a name out of place and out of time. It might work in a thirty-year-old Hollywood musical, or attached to a man of a certain age, but here in drizzly grey-skied southern England, autumn sucking the last of the leaves from the trees before the gardeners blow them under the fences into the next-door garden, it feels like someone somewhere is making a joke which you (and maybe she) are not part of.

My old English teacher would have been apoplectic about that paragraph finishing with the word 'of'. Dear Mr Wilberforce, where are you now? Is the nurse treating you kindly or are you up to your neck (over your head, more like) in more earth-bound pursuits? But I digress – such is the right of a man in my position, leaving a letter which probably won't explain anything despite beginning with the best intentions.

Sandy had disappointed her parents young, when the blonde hair she was born with turned a deep brown and thereby made her name ridiculous. Quite what she was thinking when she applied for the job I shall never understand. Clearly over-qualified, I hired her on the spot and she performed her role with aplomb, no doubt adding further disappointment for her poor parents at her low-status career. What had happened to the child who would look after them in their dotage, maybe by building the grandparent-extension to the house for free baby-sitting while the going was good, before the flow of care would reverse? Well, that child had escaped overseas to a menial spinster career of housekeeping – general drudgery spiced with occasional yearning towards the conventional life she had rejected.

She hated me fairly early on, sticking around out of perverse fascination and enjoyment of the disproportionate salary. She was not a great conversationalist at dinner, nor did her cooking extend far beyond the placing of ready-meals in the microwave. She was a serial abuser of my telephone, a regular to international and premium-rate numbers, often racking up charges beyond the end of the conversation due to her difficulty with replacing the handset correctly. Being out of the city, with poor mobile phone reception, she had insisted early on unfettered access to the landline and I was unable to refuse her anything.

In those days, she was all that I wanted in my life. I offered her marriage but she politely declined. She was marvellous with the children on the weekends when Pearl saw fit to bring them to stay. They liked her much more than me and, when Pearl reneged on the agreement, when the visits became shorter and more infrequent, it was Sandy who insisted I threaten court orders.

It was so very hard to say no to Sandy. So I said yes and then didn't do it. I'd contacted the lawyers, I'd say. Our court date has been moved, I'd say. Probably best if you don't attend, I'd say. I had a wonderful lunch at a very expensive restaurant on the day I told her I was going to the hearing. The steak was pink, the wine was red, the truffles... were there truffles? What would they have been served with? There I go again – I hear Wilberforce's voice echoing in my ear as that blasted hanging preposition blights another sentence. You could do so much better, he would say, but you're sloppy and you're lazy and you're... Who cares what you think, Wilberforce – you're probably dead.

I told her I had lost, that I didn't have the appetite to fight it in a higher court and that we shouldn't mention it to Pearl as I was sick of the subject. Sandy was very well behaved, permitted herself only glares when Pearl wasn't looking, otherwise all smiles. The frequency of the visits continued to decline. Finally Pearl emigrated and took the children with her – was it Australia or Austria? I find it hard to remember and harder to care. The children have never looked me up although Sandy told me they were far too young to do so. They would have found a way, I told her. Children are smart, I told her. They clearly care nothing for me, I told her, and I will not talk about this again.

She talked about it again and I told her I would investigate and find out about my rights and establish contact. Maybe one day I will – it has been some years, I forget how long. I am forgetting myself, but perhaps they will read this one day. If so, hello children – I loved you as best I could but there were so many more important things that I had to get done. I am not sorry but, if it helps you, I could probably have put on a good show of being sorry if you had ever come to visit me.

The work is important – not just to me, what sort of solipsist do you take me for? (Be still, Wilberforce, oh unquiet spirit.) I delve, I reach, I experiment, I write it all up carefully, I send it to my peers in the international community for their opinions and advice and criticisms (positive and negative, I am not proud). Sandy occasionally helps in a secretarial capacity although she started to find the typing uncomfortable as she entered the second trimester. She said it was mine, I didn't see how it could be but went along with her fantasy. Honestly,

I don't know how she found the time to get herself knocked-up, given the workload in the house but I can't accept the immaculate conception alternative.

I considered firing her – or at the very least reducing her salary – and recruiting a new assistant, someone who would be able to help and wouldn't grumble as much and maybe could get their own little studio-flat somewhere in town, close enough to be able to come when the work demanded it but a lot further away than Sandy stomping around in her attic bedroom when she was neither needed nor wanted about the place.

I advertised. Four men responded and, being a fair man, I interviewed them all. One of them spent too much time flattering Sandy – under the pretext of finding out about what the job entailed, he praised the elegance of her systems, the flair in her filing, the macros in her spreadsheets. I asked him if he was the father of her child, he left quickly, which I took as an admission of guilt – she was clearly trying to smuggle him into the household, perhaps the two of them would steal my work from under me. Two of the others had beards and the last cycled – I asked them why they had bothered to respond to my advertisement when clearly they had no interest or they would have made more effort.

I knuckled down and got on with my work alone. Sandy alternated bedroom stomping with days out, ostensibly to art galleries and coffee shops, although I neither knew nor cared whether that was the truth of the matter. I was reaching a breakthrough and had no time for her moods and requirements.

One afternoon the police visited. Sandy had some bruising from a trifling accident and some interfering do-gooder had informed the authorities. She told them it was nonsense, I told them I had better things to be doing with my time. The policewoman (more like police-girl if you ask me) had the temerity to ask me what those things would be. I refused to answer, but in a jovial manner, not that she would crack a smile. She suggested that she could caution me although, given that I had done nothing wrong, I told her that she was talking nonsense. No offence had been committed, I said disarmingly, so how could anyone be cautioned for anything?

She wrote many words on her pad and handed me a form to sign. I refused to do so. She said I would be hearing in due course whether the matter would be taken further. Given that I shred most letters – the accountant received the important financial ones directly – I was not too concerned about this and, indeed, nothing more was forthcoming, as far as I am aware. Well, nothing more was forthcoming regarding that matter.

A few weeks later, or perhaps it was a couple of months – I remember it was a very warm night, which suggests summer but does not help to narrow it down any more precisely than somewhere betwixt May and September. It was chilly when the police-girl visited, although that could have been any time of the year. Anyway, I had worked until very late. I lay in bed, eyes open, mind racing, unable to still my thoughts, to stop them planning the next few stages of the project. I had made great steps that week and wanted to push ahead but the flesh must be rested, even if the mind will not have it.

I developed a craving for crème brûlée. Perhaps it was nostalgia for my university days, trying to bring back at least an olfactory essence of those days of gowns and candle-lit hall dinners and undergraduates occasionally setting their hair on fire while sipping cheap wine and clumsily flirting.

I will admit, this is not the simplest craving to satisfy at around three in the morning. The previous week, I had purchased a cook's blow-torch but, frankly, found it rather disappointing. The flame was small, it burnt through the butane cannister quickly and it took far too long to brown the pudding. That week I upgraded to a plumber's blow-torch but had not had a chance to test it on sugared custard.

As I have said, it was a balmy night and I padded downstairs to stand, naked, in the kitchen, cooling myself by the open fridge while stirring the custard mixture on the hob at arm's length. Finally, I decanted it into six ramekins and generously sprinkled the coarsely granulated golden sugar over them.

A twist and click locked the gas cannister into

place. A squeeze on the trigger produced the flame, a good long blue tongue licking the tops of the puddings which quickly darkened under it. Unfortunately, my foot slipped slightly on the wet tiled floor and my aim faltered and I partially incinerated a dish cloth which someone had left lying on the counter-top. I had told Sandy time and again that the correct place for dish cloths was over the radiator, when wet, or over the little pull-out rail cleverly nestling between two cupboards, when dry, but dump them on the side she still did.

After a tantalising couple of minutes during which I thought I had got away with it, the smoke alarm finally roused itself into a squeal, which roused Sandy fairly quickly – even two stories below her, I could make out her heavy footfalls on the wooden boards of her attic room.

Surprisingly, it also roused a shirtless man who appeared behind me. More concerned to protect my work, my property and my home than my dignity, I turned towards him, squeezed the trigger again and confronted him with the full-frontal assault of my nakedness and my fire. I threw in a primeval yawl for good measure. He froze, eyes widened, mouth flapping in slack-jawed inability to think of anything to say.

I saw Sandy walking down the stairs behind him and, eager to protect her from becoming embroiled in my battle with this would-be semi-naked agent of industrial espionage, I ran at him, holding my flamethrower aloft. He turned and ran for the front door. Being faster than I, and nimble of finger, he managed to loose the chains, twist the lock and vanish into the night before I could even remark on his lack of footwear in addition to his lack of shirt, let alone scorch his buttocks.

Sandy denied that he had been in her room, declared that he must have been a burglar, swore blind that he was not the father of her unborn child and, having said her piece, began to waddle off to bed. In that case, I responded, I must telephone the police for they must investigate this attempted burglary, this breaking and entering, this dirty trick that my competitors in the industry are playing.

If you must, she responded, but do remember to put some clothes on before they come.

The police-girl who attended might have been the one I saw previously, she might not, I do find they all look so alike; either way, she either was a different child or did not recognise me or saw fit, perhaps through learned professionalism, not to mention our earlier meeting. She found a pair of shoes and a shirt in the front garden, perhaps thrown down from Sandy's attic window, perhaps discarded by the burglar on his way in. (Steady, Wilberforce...) The shoes I can understand – but the shirt? I'm just off to do a bit of burgling, but it's hot so I'll dump half of my clothes in the front garden?! I think not.

Realising that the majority of people, being of far

lower intellect than I, have a remarkably more care-free life not knowing what they do not know and not trying to answer other people's difficult questions, I did not attempt to make the investigation any easier by proffering my interpretation of the clothes anomaly. I dunno, I told her. The police-girl appeared satisfied with my lack of views and content to have another unsolved case to pass on to the nearest filing cabinet when she returned to the station. She left at the first opportunity, having given me her daytime colleague's card and a crime reference number for insurance purposes.

I took the stairs two at a time and proceeded to have a tête-à-tête with Sandy regarding the acceptability, or otherwise, of her entertaining male friends with whatever depravity she gets up to in the middle of the night. She responded that she had initially assumed he was with me, since both of us were lacking the full shilling of clothing, and that she thought we were concocting some post-coital fancy nibbles. Needless to say I was furious at this insinuation, left her room and slammed the door shut. Then, my dander still up and in a fit of pique, I went downstairs to my study, took the large keyring from my desk drawer, went back upstairs and locked her in.

Each internal door in my house has a five-lever mortice lock, certified to some British standard or other, not because I have aspirations to running a jail but because, some years ago, when I began my research, I wanted the ability to safely deposit work-in-progress in any room of the house without risk of interference by innocent child's hands or duplicitous adult fingers. I did not bother to assess each room to determine whether I was likely to need it for storage, I simply hired a locksmith and told him to get on with it. I had already acquired the locks myself from the hardware store since I saw no need to pay him his outrageous mark-up on the goods, considering the amount he charged for two day's work to be a sufficiently generous remuneration.

I suspect that Sandy was unaware that her door could be locked. She rattled the door but I quickly went downstairs and slept in the children's room so that I would not be under her room. Her voice was easily lost in the thick walls, floor, ceiling of the house and the thumping on the floor was faint enough to ignore as I drifted off to sleep. I found the singed dish-cloth the following morning and threw away the ramekins of crème brûlée as the flies had been at them. The dishwasher did not achieve much with the custard pan so I left it by the sink for Sandy.

Where was she? I wondered to myself, before fully remembering the events of the night and deciding that the quiet was joyful and perhaps she could have another few hours of considering her conduct alone before I released her.

The previous night's unpleasantries had probably

affected me more than I was willing to admit to myself and I was sorely tempted, albeit briefly, to abandon my work, to destroy my notes and experiments, to deprive this grubby, ungrateful and undeserving mass of humanity of the great advances that I could have given them. This feeling did not last for long. When the world is against one – either in reality or in one's own mind, it matters little – one can turn inwards for shelter, or one can turn outwards in a show of comradeship and generosity (any other approach is intellectually aberrant). I am fortunate in being able to turn inwards towards my work which I shall, soon I hope, be able to give to the world, thereby fulfilling both options simultaneously.

Leaving the custard pan without so much as a backward glance, I headed into my study, calmed my mind by revisiting the notes I had made prior to the crème brûlée debâcle and carried on my struggle.

It had been Pearl who advised me to contact a patent agent. Some of your work is brilliant, she had said, even though I knew for a fact that she had little idea about what I was working on. (Wilberforce, I find you a tiresome presence and I am now leaving these hanging prepositions just to annoy you. Just so you know – I'm doing, on purpose, something you cannot put up with.) The man duly arrived, buttoned up in a cheap suit, emerging from a car with its idle speed set too high, a child seat strapped into the back, a faded music festival sticker left inside the windscreen – in short, a man with whom I could have nothing in common. Normally I like it that way – it prevents small-talk by giving nothing to oil that slack wheel and yet, a man to whom I could describe my life's work – surely he should be one cut from the same cloth as I?

He found no merit in my work and advised me that there was little originality which would be worth the filing fees, the adviser fees, the agent fees, the appeal fees. Obviously he did not phrase it as simply as that – his demurral was dressed up in flim-flam and nonsensical verbiage, phrases like 'not as such' instead of 'no', words like 'extraordinary' when he clearly wanted to say 'rubbish'.

It was a happier time in my life and I merely smiled at his lack of understanding and told him that I bore no hard feelings, that I appreciated his time and his input and his honesty. I shook his hand and sent him on his way, giving him some advice of my own, namely that he should have his car serviced to stop it burning so much fuel unnecessarily. He responded with a thin smile and over-revved and understeered his way out of my driveway onto the lane that rejoins the main road. I was not sufficiently generous to tell him that if he had turned the other way onto the lane, he could have avoided joining the dual carriageway the wrong way, given that the earliest turning opportunity is three miles away and very close to a school that would have been kicking out around that time.

I found myself wondering, that day after the crème brûlée debâcle, whether I should invite him to come back, show him how far I had come, explain it all again just to see if he would get it this time. If nothing else, I was curious to discover whether he still had the same car, to hear whether it still laboured unnecessarily, to see whether there were now two child seats. It had been very long ago, I thought – would the children still need the booster seats? Would they have left home? I find the passage of time a slippery beast and, when I found my notes from those years ago and dialled the number of his agency, I found it was no longer the number of a patent agency. The uninterested lady who spoke to me either could not or would not tell me anything about whence they might have gone – or perhaps I am being too generous in not merely interpreting her demeanour as vacant.

The standards of education seem to have slumped in inverse proportion to the greed of those recently ejected from the process. Graduates sniff at the idea of anything less than an accelerated promotion scheme, while those leaving school at the first opportunity seem to think the world owes them a huge income as a rapper or some such talentless profession. Even people old enough and rich enough to know better become apoplectic due to their greed and stupidity. A few weeks ago, a man was haranguing a sales assistant for the sin of reimbursing his parking charge by reducing the bill to the credit card rather than returning the cash. What about my cashback on my card? The man waved the card, rather nearer to the lowly-paid man's face than common courtesy would countenance. I seized his wrist, much to his surprise (and mine, truth be told) and pointed out that the difference in cashback which he would receive in a few months would amount to exactly one penny per visit to the store. Amazingly, this did not stop him as he foamed on with the rejoinder that they were his pennies, not anyone else's.

Does humanity even deserve the fruits of my research, my experimentation, the years of struggle? Some days my nose itches to smell the bonfire. I can almost hear the crackle.

I awoke with a start, thinking I could smell smoke, but the olfactory misfire faded as I shook off the doziness. It was now dark outside but, as I seldom wear a watch and do not allow clocks into my work rooms, I was unsure of the time. The door was shut, my work was laid out beautifully before me, there was absolute silence, the chair was comfortable, I had all that I needed. I smiled, leaned forward, lay my forearms on the desk, and rested my head on them. I closed my eyes again.

Back when the children were small, Pearl and I rationed the television they could watch. We purchased discs of programmes we had loved as

children and indeed then enjoyed again as adults,
sitting alongside wide-eyed wonder, revelling in the
few minutes of calm and rapt attention. The modern
programmes won out in the end. Peer pressure saw
to that, although we managed to resist the premium
children's channels for many years – goodness
knows how ostracised our children might have
become if we had stood firm as far as their teenage
years.

I wondered if I still had the discs, or whether
Pearl took them. Perhaps the children would gain
respect from their peers by bringing them to
university. Were they university age yet? I couldn't
remember. Anyway, I thought that if I still had the
discs, maybe I could watch them with Sandy and
her child. Maybe I should lock the work away in
one of the attic rooms, move Sandy onto the proper
upstairs, redecorate one of the children's rooms as a
nursery, goodness me, not do it myself – get
someone in! Maybe I should ask her to marry me
again, but try to sound like I mean it this time.
Maybe I could do better with this child than with the
others. Is it mine? Were they? Does it matter?

And I was reminded that I hadn't seen her that
day, just as I dozed off again. It was light when I
awoke.

There was no getting away from it – Sandy
would be angry by now. How many days had it
been? Only one, surely, although keeping track of
the passage of time was never my strong suit.

Wilberforce hated that phrase, I can almost hear him now telling us that life is not just a pack of cards. I wonder how he would have handled releasing Sandy from her attic room after a day's imprisonment. Although, that's the local paper being put through the door, and that only happens on a Friday, and the day of the crème brûlée debâcle was... which must mean...

I can't remember how long it's been since I last heard the stomping on the floor, and the faint plaintive sounds have petered out. Maybe she has escaped through the window, and scuttled down the wall and fled into the autumnal woodland. I expect that is what has happened. Really there is no need to look – there's no way a resourceful girl like Sandy would have put up with being locked up. (Too many 'up's, booms Wilberforce's ghost.) She must have gone, so the child will not be born here – she will probably have shacked up with her shirtless burglar, I wouldn't be surprised if there's another one on the way.

I do miss her. Post still arrives for her occasionally and it reminds me that Sandy lived here for a while.

Head Stand Ascension

Stand on your head.

She had turned, bent forwards, placed her hands flat on the ground, stared at him from between her knees, her ears brushing against the graze, her hair tickling her shins. He had asked her to do that, she had smiled, her hand instinctively reaching for penguin unaccountably lost three days earlier, the automatic grasping stymied by the absence, fingers widening their search before the lip quivered, the upside-down face giving the upside-down smile, the tears beginning to run up the forehead.

The sight of her distress almost stopped him.

She was convinced that he had risen, that her father had experienced his own ascension. On the good days, she truly believed that he had been pulled as though on silken ropes by a choir of heavenly angels. On the bad days, she knew he had risen but decided it was of his own volition, he was escaping her, he was taking his place with the righteous, for even those who run away can be righteous.

He had not made a sound, and neither had she.

No one came running for no one thought they needed to. Women smiled at her, men averted their eyes lest they be accused of improper thought. Finally, a man in a uniform, gun in its holster, asked her where her mom or her pop were at. Her mum, she said, was at home and her daddy had flown away into the sky after climbing that fence. She pointed, his eyes widened, he took out his radio but the body was never found. Of course it wasn't, she would say later and the following year and through the decades that followed. How could it be found in the gorge when it had gone up? They should have scrambled the helicopters, not the climbers with their ropes and harnesses to see if he had snagged on the way down; they should have sent fighter jets looking for him, not the jeep on the thirty-mile round trip to the bottom to comb through the gorse and grasses.

He's gone to look for penguin, she decided, and she told to the man with the gun, and to the woman who came running from the shed and who scooped her up and carried her back and made strange cooing noises and said that everything would be all right, which clearly it wouldn't as she knew that penguin hadn't flown up into the sky because penguins can't fly. But then, neither can fathers, not normally. We'll get your mommy, said the woman, although it was three days before her mummy arrived because she had to fly to so many wrong places first: connections, as the woman said and she had nodded because the woman made it sound important.

When will daddy come back with penguin, she asked when her mummy arrived, finally, and held her in her arms and squeezed her so hard she couldn't finish her question but that didn't matter because mummy didn't answer it anyway, nor did she answer it the second time she asked, with the rest of the question put back where it belonged. When will daddy come back with penguin and can he live with us again?

She still has the replacement penguin which her mummy bought from the airport shop two days later. With no body and no witness to the death (other than a distraught little girl – I'm not distraught, she said), he could only be classed as a missing person, which saved the trouble of the repatriation and the inquest and the coroner, and meant that there was nothing to stop them from returning home.

Thirty-four years later she found the photographs from the trip when she was clearing out her mother's attic. She was not surprised that her mother hadn't shown her the pictures before, although she wouldn't have expected her to have had them developed in the first place. It dawned on her, gradually enough that she rebuked herself for being slow on the uptake, that this must have meant that the camera was still in the hotel room, which meant that he didn't take it that day, which meant that he was planning his departure, so the angels did not suddenly pluck him from the face of the planet – he rose by his own choice, and at the time of his choosing.

She was angry with him for not telling her – never mind that she had been a four-year-old child – he should have found a way of telling her, or left a note in the hotel room. She deserved an explanation.

When she came back the following week for another expedition into the loft, she found the papers. Why do you only go once a week, her husband asked her. I'll help you, we'll leave Max with my parents, we'll spend a weekend and we'll deal with it all and you won't have it hanging over you and we can sell the house and you can move on.

I can't, she said. One hour, once a week, that's as much as I can give, you're just trying to save the council tax and the insurance. I couldn't care less about the council tax or the insurance, he said, I want you back. But I only spend one hour a week there, she said and smiled. But you're not properly with us the rest of the time, he said.

The note was an apology without an explanation. The other papers were for the missed hospital appointments due to his being 'missing' (or 'dead', as his ex-wife would attest; or 'risen', as his daughter saw it). Even with the medicine of three decades ago it was treatable, so his condition was no explanation for his seeking help from a higher authority, he who healeth the sick, apparently.

He didn't kill himself, she would argue with her mother as the decades rolled around and her mother's hair turned brown to grey to white, he ascended. Her mother could only snort and turn up the volume on the television as she had run out of ways to argue the point. And then last year she had pulled out of the argument for good.

Jessica is still angry with her mother and the anger leaks out in her disproportionate retaliation to the simplest and most innocent slights. She notes down number plates of cars who block her driveway, even by an inch, when their drivers or passengers visit the doctor across the street. The first time, they get away with it. The second time, a polite note is slid under the windscreen wiper. The third time, a strongly worded note is glued to the windscreen – just children's glue, officer, easily washed off. The fourth time, a bombardment with whatever overripe fruit comes to hand. She watches the bewilderment, the fury, the foot-stamping, the colourful language from behind her net curtains, sitting still so that her movement will not betray her.

On the bad days, she waits by the car and unleashes her rage, giving no quarter for apology, confusion, disability, pregnancy or even a disarming smile.

"Did you talk to anyone today?" asks Daniel, once he has come home and slipped off his shoes and kissed her and kissed Max and sat down for dinner.

"Yes," she says. "Max and I have been chatting all afternoon, haven't we Max?"

"I don't like this," says Max, using his spoon to push food off his fork.

Earlier that afternoon, Max had tightened his grip on her hand and tugged her as her voice rose in the toyshop. Louder and louder she was getting, the consonants crisper, the vowels converging as her home town began to exert itself in her accent. The target was not the woman who had interrupted their purchase in the toyshop in order to quickly buy a pack of batteries because she had a little girl with Downs over there and she might run out of the shop so she had to be quick. Jessica did not ask, icily, why the woman couldn't simply hold her child's hand and wait in the queue like everybody else. Jessica turned her stare onto the sales assistant and asked her why she had served the woman and why that woman with her incompetent control of her child should be allowed to jump queues and surely, if the sales assistants would just tell her to sling her hook, then she, and the countless hordes of soi-disant entitlees might realise it was time to shut their stupid traps and queue up like normal decent people did.

Max does not want to mention that to daddy as he has told daddy before when mummy was angry and mummy just got angry again, not with him and not with daddy – just angry thinking about it but, once she was angry, she could lash out at either of them. He shouldn't mention it. He's hidden the new toy train under his bed so daddy doesn't see it and ask when he got it because then he would have to talk about the toy shop. He'll leave it a few days and then he can just say he's had it for ages and can't remember who gave it to him and then he could ask daddy for the batteries which mummy had forgotten to buy, which was funny because Max thought that having the argument with the lady buying batteries might have reminded her.

"How was nursery?" asks Daniel.

"Fine," says Max."

"What did you do this morning?"

"I've forgotten."

Max hasn't forgotten the moment when Sammy said that her grandfather was picking her up today and Max said that his grandfather had been picked up himself, all the way up into the sky and Miss Susan smiled and said things like "there there" and Max said that he wasn't sad because his grandfather wasn't dead – mummy had said he was up in the sky somewhere, that he'd wanted to be up there. Miss Susan had had a chat with mummy when she came to collect him and he'd played with Miss Poppy and couldn't quite hear the words they were saying but he could hear the quiet fury in mummy's voice and he didn't ask her on the way home what they'd been talking about.

Max likes to run. He holds Brian's hand and the

little bear flaps against his leg as he tears along the pavement, mummy shouting at him to stop but he thinks it's a game and he's laughing as he runs and she's wearing the wrong shoes but she runs after him anyway and grabs him around the wrist and tugs sharply so his left foot goes up in the air and he spins around on his right and nearly tumbles over but she's holding him up. He stops laughing when he sees the look on her face, even though she's smiling and saying nice things, at this moment he's frightened of her, even though she's picking him up and pulling him tight into her and he tucks his feet around her waist and tries to pull Brian out from where he's trapped between his knee and her side.

A traffic warden nearby has been watching, paused in preparing a ticket for a badly parked car, one wheel up on the kerb, one wheel on a double-yellow, two wheels in a bay, windscreen missing any sort of permit.

"It's not my car," she snaps at him.

"Just getting ready to catch him if he tripped," he says, startling her. They don't normally talk to you, she thinks.

"No need."

"Or ran into the road."

"I've taught him better than that. Anyway, nice to see you ticketing these selfish people for a change. I saw one of you lot phoning for a clamp for a car wrapped round a tree last week. Driver died, I heard. And while you're here, the tax has expired on that silver car up the road."

Jessica gave Max her replacement penguin when they returned home and he thanked her and took it to his room, saying he wanted to introduce it (her, corrected his mummy) to the other toys. He pushed it into the pile of bears, covered it up, especially covered the nasty hard plastic eyes and the place on the left side of the face where the bristly fur had worn away.

Max hugged Brian tight against his chest, the top of its head a soft comfort against his throat. I'll never lose you, he mouthed to the bear, silently, in case the penguin was listening, even though he knew they were both only toys. He looked up to check whether the penguin was spying on him and saw that it had managed to work one of its wings loose, it was sticking out – but he didn't mind the wings so much, it looked like it was growing out of Cedric the white teddy, he liked the idea of being able to fly away, just like granddad had all those years ago.

But he didn't want to look at any more of penguin because it would make him think of mummy and even though he loved her and would call her or run to her in the middle of the night if he was frightened or couldn't get to sleep or just felt lonely in his bed, he didn't want to just be lying there looking at her penguin and thinking about her. The thought of her could be terrifying in the dark. She was always so angry, and the smile she used to cover the anger was so thin and so easily cracked and the anger leaked out through her eyes and the clenching of her fingers and the tap-tap-slide of mild tooth-grinding.

Jessica taps her fingers and clenches her teeth as she thinks back, as she tries to picture her father as he was then, as she tries to remember what they were doing the day before he left her, or the day before that, or where she last saw penguin. She has the photographs now but she does not see herself in the girl posing uncomfortably against a viewpoint or a wall, clearly mid-fidget, maybe her father wasn't the fastest at framing his pictures. She does not know where any of the pictures were taken, there is nothing written on the back but then again, she thinks, who would have been doing the writing?

She has nothing of the trip in her memory, her recollections are all of her mother talking to her about it or, more usually, refusing to talk about it. She struggles to picture her father next to her on the plane as they flew out there – she can make up a picture in her mind but the image of him is wrong, her mind has appropriated it from her parents' wedding photograph, or from the colour-drained shot of him chasing her on the beach, the old small matt-finish picture over-saturated with orange and brown. The man sitting next to her on the jet was not in his swimming trunks, nor was he wearing a navy jacket and a narrow tie. How had they travelled? Had he hired a car? Had it been buses or trains? Had he known anyone out there? Could she track down the friend, if there had been such a person, could she find him or her? What would she ask even if she could? Why did he do it? What sort of answer could she expect? After three decades of asking her mother, did she want to spend time tracking down a phantom to continue the questioning? Although, she concedes to herself with a smile, who better to ask about a ghost than a phantom?

She teaches Max to stand on his head.

"Won't it hurt if I put my shoe on my head?"

No, silly. Stand like this, put your hands there, look between your knees. When you're older, you can try kicking your legs up against a wall.

"Everything is upside down." He stands up and walks into her bedroom, tries it in front of her mirrored wardrobe. "Everything is upside down but I'm not. Why?"

She tries to explain about turning something upside down twice but gets bogged down and he loses interest and fidgets and she can't stand the fidgeting and the not concentrating so she just walks away, in the middle of her own sentence and she knows that she wants to stay and laugh and hug him and play with him and enjoy him and be everything that her father was before he went away but her legs don't stop walking away and downstairs and as far away as she can get inside the house, all the way through the kitchen to the back door where she stares at the garden and wonders whether Daniel will mow the grass before it becomes taller than Max. There is silence from upstairs. She doesn't know what Max is doing and she wants to call to him but can't think of which words she should use so she doesn't use any. She opens the door and steps outside and softly closes it behind her so that, if he starts crying, she won't be able to hear; so that, if she starts crying, he won't be able to hear.

Sirens go past the house, accompanied by the scrape of the lowered bumper as the car bucks over the speed hump. Jessica remembers the policeman taking her away from her father's launch-site. He wore his hat in the car. He turned and smiled, showed her his good straight bright teeth. He said, shall we drive fast and put the woo-woo on. She asked if he meant the siren. He laughed and told her she was a clever little pretty little thing and the car lurched forward and he flicked a switch and the noise started. Are you allowed to drive that fast, she asked him. He laughed again, turned and winked, his teeth glinted as he said, "Ain't no one gonna stop me, I'm the police," except he actually said poh-lease, he milked the word for its full two syllables.

She wonders if the car driving past the house is answering an emergency call, hurtling to the rescue, taking its driver into confrontation and danger, or whether the driver is just another policeman showing off to a girl.

She wonders how she can contact that poh-lease-man, whether he can tell her anything after all this time, whether he is still alive or maybe has been killed in a car accident, or a shoot-out with a dangerous man or has just keeled over and been taken out by natural causes. Even if he is still alive he wouldn't remember anything at all about me, she decides, and the records would be in a cardboard box on a high shelf in a room full of boxes and shelves which is visited once every few years to no avail at the request of people like her. She decides that the poh-lease force has more important and urgent matters to attend to.

When Max is at nursery and Daniel is at work and, now that her mother can no longer answer her calls, Jessica often talks to Brian. The line of stitching representing the mouth gives the toy a benevolent, wise yet placid appearance. The twin circles of black thread for the eyes are easy to gaze into. He is a good listener as she frets and flirts, agonises and antagonises.

"Penguin's buried under the bears again, Brian. I don't think Max likes her."

"Daniel's work was supposed to have calmed down last month – why is he still getting home so late, Brian?"

"Now, Brian, where did you hide the car keys?"

"What shall we have for dinner, Brian?"

"Brian, do you think I can make it to the pool for a swim before picking up Max?"

"I'm not sure if Daniel will notice my new black strappy shoes if I wear them on Saturday. What do you think, Brian?"

"What happened to my daddy, Brian?"

Brian is always arranged carefully for Max's return from nursery. Some days, he is pressed against the window, arm up to shade his eyes from sunlight. Other days he is tucked up in bed, sometimes with penguin but normally with another toy. Max squawks his infant laugh and rushes to grab his bear, sometimes trying to coax him down from a ledge with a handful of imaginary food, sometimes just hooking him with the handle of his rainbow umbrella.

A few weeks before they spoke for the last time, Jessica's mother told her about the time immediately after her father's death (he didn't die!).

"They told me you asked for penguin, then you said daddy would be back soon, then finally you asked for me."

Jessica was furious. "Am I supposed to feel bad about what someone told you that I might have said when I was four? Why weren't you there anyway?"

"I don't want to talk about it."

"Well isn't that a surprise. Another thing about my damaged childhood which you don't want to tell me about. Had you two split up? Did you just tell him you didn't want to go so you could flit around art galleries and try to get yourself a fancy man?" She said 'fancy man' in a quiet pastiche-upper-class accent.

"You don't need to adopt that tone with me."

"Well, I've tried every other tone I can think of and you never explain anything. Did I tell you I've started reading philosophy? Did you know that Seneca thought that the root of anger was hope? That must be why I'm so angry all the time – I live in hope! I hope that daddy comes back. I hope you tell me what happened all those years ago. I hope I don't screw up Max's childhood the way you destroyed mine."

After that, she didn't need to slam the door on the way out of her mother's kitchen; in many ways the gentle click of the catch was more contemptuous. There was no note with the will, nothing to set her mind at rest. There could be enlightenment buried amongst the boxes and bags and clutter in the loft but she has yet to discover it.

Daniel normally falls asleep before her. She stares at him, lying there peacefully, lying there without a care in the world, lying there gently snuffling. Some nights she smiles with contentment and snuggles further down under the duvet. Most nights the tears come and she doesn't understand why and without understanding why, how can she fix the problem? She has a comfortable life doesn't she? She has a well-appointed house and a well-respected husband and a well-socialised child but it is never enough.

She lies awake as the tears come and she thinks of the less fortunate, the whole wide range of the less fortunate from the mothers outside nursery complaining about their husbands' car choices to the truly deprived elsewhere on the planet but none of this makes her feel any better. There are those who suffer more but everyone's misery is relative to their situation.   Perhaps those who struggle for food could not understand how one could be miserable with a full belly but that did not invalidate the way that she felt. Never having to go without gifted her mind the luxury of exploring the misery of her unsatisfactory life, the frustration of not knowing why she feels the yawning emptiness and futility of her existence, the guilt of being so ungrateful for her many and various blessings.

In her irrational moments she wishes for a life wholly occupied with walking several miles to fetch water, using every part of any meat or fish or vegetable or pulse which she could afford, stitching and darning and letting out and taking in clothes to get every last day's wear from them. Anything, she feels, would be better than the rage, the night tears, the frustration while waiting for her father to come back with penguin.

"We should go to the museum at the weekend," says Daniel. He doesn't need to say which one, he has been promising it regularly, every two or three weeks, for the past few months but each Thursday or, sometimes, cruelly, late on Friday, he discovers that his workplace cannot spare him for the Saturday and so he dutifully travels to the office and leaves a fuming Jessica placating a truculent, disappointed Max.

"Oh really? Is it going to happen this time?"

"Yes," says Daniel and he apologises and explains that the project finished three days ago and the client has agreed and the documents are as good as signed and the partners have as good as uncorked the champagne and the weekend is as good as his.

However, late on Friday, the partners were as good as pushing the corks back into the bottles and signatures were being struck through and the client had changed its contract negotiators and, even though to anyone outside the business, the deal was a matter of utmost triviality, it nevertheless had to be completed to everyone's satisfaction before the markets opened on Monday. Max is already in bed, curled up with Brian, far away from penguin, when Daniel returns home. His head is stooped and he examines the sock fluff caught in the carpet as Jessica informs him that she and Max will be going anyway and maybe, just maybe, they'll let him come with them if they ever decide to go again. She is fully calm and softly spoken, using the tone, he thinks, that she would adopt if she were to be talking to him while bludgeoning him with a small item of furniture.

"But why isn't daddy coming?" asks Max, his gaze everywhere around the station platform, on her bag, at the poster of the silver-haired man extolling the virtues of a brand of coffee, on her bag again, at the lady with bright red hair half-way down the platform.

"He has to work," she says, smiling and suddenly realising that it is a genuine smile, that she feels happy to be taking her son on a treat, an adventure. She doesn't have to share him at the weekend, she is dispensing fun and he will love her for it. She knows that the day will end with Max being overtired and grumpy and probably crying or even screaming at her but she pushes that thought to one side. She thinks about her philosophy course and decides that, for as long as she can manage it, she will live in the moment today and enjoy the present and deal with the future when she gets to it and ignore the past and all its imperfections. All the best days end with screaming, Daniel would say but he's not here today and she's not going to be saying that herself, not yet anyway.

Max is still staring at her bag. She has brought the large bag – it is far too big for the few things she has inside it but she wanted to buy something for Max in the shop and maybe find a postcard or a trinket for herself and, if she's feeling generous, which she intends to be, she'll find something for Daniel, perhaps a tie or a ridiculous ornament for his desk at work. She follows his gaze and realises that the zip is not fully shut.

She takes the bag off her shoulder. Max lunges for it and pulls the zip and in goes his hand and out comes Brian.

"Well," she says, "we have a stowaway! I

wonder how he got there."

"He wanted to come with us," said Max, his thumb nearing his mouth as his self-control fights against his instinct to suck the thumb. The instinct wins and the bear is tucked under the arm as he reaches for her hand with his free, dry hand.

A distant rumbling from the tunnel, Max turns towards the sound and adjusts his hold on his mother's hand and his elbow moves imperceptibly and Brian slides out onto the floor where he meets the shoe of a man in a grey suit who is reaching into his pocket and not entirely watching where he is placing his feet. His toe slams silently into Brian's side. Brian slides effortlessly across the platform to the edge where he slows, teeters and then drops.

"Mummy! Brian!"

"Don't worry, Max."

"Brian!"

She looks over the edge, expecting to see the bear lying in the black dust between rails and sleepers. It can be laundered, she thinks. It will never be the same colour again, she thinks. Someone will be able to retrieve it, she thinks. She spots Brian balanced across a rail. She does not know whether it is the live rail, she cannot remember how to tell them apart.

"Stand back from the platform edge," booms the announcer. It does not sound like the usual recording – there is a greater urgency in the voice. "Madam, please stand back from the edge and control your son."

She sees the man in his silly jacket and his little hat and she waves to show that she has heard him and to show that he should stop worrying his little head in its little hat about how well she can control her child.

Max is thrashing against her to try to reach his bear. She hadn't noticed him. Penguin was gone, there was no need for Brian to be destroyed. How hard could it be? The rumbling must have been on another platform as no train has appeared. If only she had brought her umbrella, or even Max's umbrella, then she could have swept Brian up and rescued him. She grips Max firmly by the shoulders and turns him around so that he faces the wall, so that he can see the man with grey hair in the poster peddling his coffee.

"Stand on your head," she tells him, and she smiles as his face appears between his knees. "Is mummy upside down now?"

High Thumb Cuticle

He had been born Frank but preferred Francis, told everyone his name was Francis, cut people off if they ever called him Frankie, even called himself Francis when phoning his mother – "hello mother, it's Francis" – she had given up remonstrating.

He still blamed her for his affliction, as he saw it, for his disability, as he saw it, for the genes that had led to his mutation, as he saw it, which had inexorably led to his seat at the desk three rows from the window, four partitions from the door, two from the coffee machine, the desk where the work was meaningless and irrelevant, yet urgent and important and reasonably, but not extravagantly, paid. The extravagance was upstairs, where the computer screens were larger and the racket never ending and the salaries extraordinary. They'd never get their work done without him yet they were revenue and he was support – they were income-generating and he was income-sapping. He and his little team were ants to them – easily trodden on, easily replaced.

He wasn't supposed to be here – but then, who

was? What made him special – why did he deserve anything better? What right did he have to expect that he was owed respect, adulation, a detached house in a nice suburb? He couldn't answer the question that way around, but he knew – deep down he was certain – that the reason he wasn't going to get anything better (irrespective of what he deserved) and the reason he wouldn't receive respect, adulation or anything better than a studio apartment a bus ride away from the office (irrespective of what he was owed) was the same as the reason why he was special. It was working against him – what made him special was his weakness, his affliction, his disability, his mutation.

The window winked up on his screen, the instructions coming down from upstairs to reboot this and restart that. His fingers skittered and clattered over the keyboard as he sent the commands to wherever in the world the outsourced server was located this week. Francis had only been with the company for four years but he remembered when the machines were lined up in the air-purified basement of the building, when Bryan and Robbo had cared for them and nurtured them and soothed their frantically winking green and amber lights with typed messages and box-fresh slide-in slide-out disk drives. The room was now a gym, its former human inhabitants no longer required, its former electronic inhabitants taken over and taken away by the new logistics and solutions provider. The new service was rubbish, the quality-assured company having negotiated an allowed, penalty-free, two hours of crippling downtime per incident – Bryan had never exceeded twenty minutes. The management had made the astonishing discovery that a bad service was cheaper than a good service and, for having such perspicacity, they had paid themselves most generously in ongoing options and bonuses and upgraded dental cover. Francis was still paying every time the phone rang in the middle of the night, at the weekend, while he lay shivering in flu-saturated bedclothes, while he lay sand-encrusted on a Devon beach.

Only last month he had seen the man fall, he felt some urge to look out of the window, as though directed, as though he had known it would happen – what a load of claptrap, he knew, how about all the other times he had looked out of the window and nothing had happened? Last month, one morning, sitting on a bar stool, elbows on a high table by the window in the canteen, staring at a coffee and a pastry, he had suddenly looked up and his eyes had found the falling man – he looked so calm – as he glided past on his way down. Francis had made eye contact, he felt that the man raised an eyebrow in greeting, but then he was gone. Francis had not left the building for several hours, did not want to see the outcome, wanted to allow plenty of time for the pavement to be cleaned, for the police tape to be removed, for the cracked paving stone to be the only sign that something untoward may have happened although, with time, with memory fading, it would just be another slab broken, probably under the hoof of a Transit van – the road repairers breaking the pavement again.

Bob heard a rumour that the window cleaner had filed the cable, or had damaged the pulley, or had broken one of the supports. Bob had told him that the window cleaner had had a tragedy in his life and maybe wanted to end it but didn't have the bottle to see it through so left it to chance, never wanted to know when it would happen, just wanted to give a little helping hand, a little nudge.

Bob never knows what he's talking about. There must be at least four or five guys that do the windows on this building – if Bob was right, which he normally wasn't, there was more chance that the guy would take out one of his colleagues than himself. Bob addresses these objections to his own satisfaction, he says the guy was obviously loopy and hadn't thought it through. Francis knows the guy was called Russell. Bob has perfectly manicured nails. Francis bites his nails, especially his right thumb nail.

Bob is a lifer, he's been with the company since graduation and he'll sit it out till retirement or redundancy or corporate bankruptcy, whichever comes first. Sure, he'll listen to the gripes and the whinges and he'll nod like he hears you, bro, but he won't participate, he won't add any of his own

ingredients to the grumble soup, just stir whatever
you're bringing to the pan, just nod and smile and
wait and remember and bide his time, keep it
simmering, ready to boil over at the slightest tweak.
Bob knows who's happy and who's not, Bob knows
just where to stick the knife and how far he can
twist it.   Bob knows when the time is right to
entertain the troops, entertain himself, sacrifice
another goat.

Bob and Francis have almost the same phone
number, just switch the sixth and seventh digits and
you've got whichever one of them you didn't want.
More relevantly for Francis, dial Bob with clumsy
fingers and Francis is transferring you or Francis is
writing your message on his pad or Francis is
thanking you for your call but he's pretty sure Bob
isn't recruiting at the moment or looking to go on a
training course or keen to try a trendy new local
restaurant prior to booking the team Christmas
lunch or interested in a six month contract in Dubai.
Bob has never taken a message for Francis but then
Francis doesn't receive many calls.

Bob   isn't   management   material,   he's   not
interested in playing the promotion game, he won't
be upgrading his chair or getting a window-view or,
holiest of grails, getting his own door any time soon
or perhaps ever. But he'll get in early and he'll be
bright-eyed when it counts and he won't volunteer
but he won't shy away either and he'll ride it all out
and will be there when the wide-eyed young

graduates arrive and move upwards and burn out just before the next coach-load arrives.   And sometimes he'll help them towards their burn-out, sometimes with the slightest nudge and sometimes with an almighty great shove, whichever will give him the greatest amusement at the time.

Bob is such fun at parties, he can even play the guitar.

Francis started too late to play the guitar.   He didn't have the patience to wait for the skin on the pads of his fingers to harden, even the nylon strings were tougher than his resolve, steel strings were out of the question – no Nashville twang would ever thrum its way past the scuffed wallpaper of the stairwell outside his bedsit.

He started too early to play the piano.   Ever an obedient child, he tinkled through Bach and Brahms, plinked and plonked over Satie and Debussy and trilled Mozart as he passed Grades 1, 2 and 3.   Too young to challenge, to ask for blues and rock and pop – frankly anything he could play to impress his friends on the odd occasion they found themselves in a room containing a piano.   Even the trombonists had it better than him – after the first lesson they could make a farting noise.

Come on Frankie, the numbskulls had chorused one afternoon when the music teacher was late and the piano was waiting, its lid up, its yellowed and chipped keys way past the best-before date when they might have gleamed – yet still inviting, still starting that itch in Francis to just get up there and show them, to show them all that he might not be any good at football or running away from bullies but he could play a tune, a good tune, a tune with a glissando.

The glissando, the coolest piano trick, the hand gliding up and down the keys, the thumb-nail clacking into each hard white (or yellowed) edge as the piano sang a violent lift-off or a thunderous splash-down – he'd never quite got one right, they jerked and spasmed up and down the octaves as he had the pressure too high and his thumb would jam against a note – or too light and the keys would clack but the hammers wouldn't reach the strings. Today would be different as, buoyed by the chanting of his name, he strode to the piano, shot his cuffs, smiled, bowed, stooped over the keys, extended his thumb, took it way up high, all the way to the top and brought it down and across as the door swung open and his cuticle snagged the thirteenth key and it bled and he cried and his reputation was in tatters and the crowd went wild with laughter and derision. Mr Taylor told him to clean the keys before taking himself off to sick-bay for a sticking plaster.

Play us a tune, Frankie – it became the playground taunt, it announced his arrival in the playground, in any classroom whose teacher was yet to arrive and, in the chemistry lesson whether the teacher was there or not.

No school band would have him so he never learnt the three-chord rock song from the sixth-formers who knotted their ties backwards so the thin part hung down and the wider side was tucked behind the shirt-front. He never learnt the blues or jazz chord progressions from the scruffier children of champagne-socialist parents. They didn't want to jam with cry-baby Frankie who could only trill Mozart. He never learnt that a pentatonic scale had nothing to do with the bible.

Fourteen years later he noticed Mike's thumb-nail. Mike had perfect pitch, he could hear a tune and play it, and he could play it on pretty much any instrument, although he didn't like the guitar but, if he really had to, if enough people said oh go on, Mike, he'd play it better than most other people in the room (regardless of the room). He could certainly play a whole lot better than Bob. Mike had a long thumb-nail, not long upwards but long downwards, the cuticle two-thirds of the way from the nail's edge to the thumb's joint. Francis had a cuticle one-third of the way down. His thumb was too short, his cuticle was too high – it all came back to that oddity, that deformity, subtle enough that he had never before noticed, yet important enough to have changed the course of his life.

And here he was, sitting at his desk like a good corporate slave, performing regular repetitive tasks for regular repetitive pay while regularly being both taken for granted and treated as though his very existence was a matter most trivial. It's not that he thought he should have been up there with his band at the MTV awards, scooping their sixth consecutive trophy for best whatever. It's that the music should have been his opportunity to build a social circle and a network of friends (never mind whether in high places) and to build self-confidence and drive and motivation and to get a better job where his opinions mattered and people listened and people sought him out to ask. Being in a second-division band, playing the smaller clubs or the larger pubs occasionally would have been great too.

His computer chirruped as an email arrived. Francis sighed in expectation of more inane triviality and was not disappointed. Fun Dilemma Of The Week! At least Bob had spelt dilemma correctly this time, Francis thought. He found it faintly pathetic that, despite spell-check running by default, auto-correction to take out the worst crimes against the English language and, if all else failed, easy access to dictionary.com, Bob still persevered in sending emails liberally littered with wrongly doubled consonants, dodgy vowels and poorly mixed word gravy. Homonyms, lousy grammar, randomly applied apostrophes – he could feel the reason why they were always present but nonsensical spelling? Someone needed to teach Bob what the wiggly red line under the words meant.

Francis double-clicked on the message.

Who is the bigger idiot? As I was walking to the
station this morning, past the usual stationary traffic,
I saw a gap between cars, maybe a gap five cars
long. Great idea, I thought, that guy is saving his
fuel by moving his car less often over greater
distances. Then some charmer in a jumped-up
Lexus shed-on-wheels from somewhere way back in
the queue pulls out onto the wrong side of the road
to pass about eight cars and slot into the space in
front of Mr Fuel Economy. Who is the bigger idiot?
The gap leaver or the gap taker? Whaddya say –
you snooze, you lose – or – wait in line like
everyone else, meat-head? But wait a minute, you
ain't got all the facts yet, sunshine. Some time later,
and bear in mind these guys are driving at around
walking pace so they go past me, I go past them, the
charade happens over and over, people, so some
time later, I see Mr Fuel Economy is still leaving
big gaps in front of him and, as I pass him, I see
why. He's texting while he drives so he has to leave
a big gap because he's not even slightly looking
where he's going. Who's the bigger idiot now?

Obviously me, thought Francis, for reading this
drivel. There go another couple of minutes of my
life I'm not getting back, he thought, before thinking
that, even by letting such a shameless cliché run
through his head, he was beginning the descent to
Bob's level. He resisted the urge to hit the reply-all
button to ask people to avoid using the reply-all
button. He tried to think back to what he was

working on as the computer pinged over and over again, signalling the arrival of each wave of hilarity in every over-inclusive reply.

Finally, it stopped. They're all sated, thought Francis, the last word has been spoken, they're all metaphorically rolling on the floor laughing. He looked around the office – no one was literally rolling on the floor laughing. Many, many desks away, Bob stood up, pushed his chair under his desk and walked slowly towards Arthur's office in the corner, the room with the view, the desk with its own walls around it and door to protect it.

Ten minutes later, a head-down sober-faced Bob opened the door to Arthur's office and slowly walked back to his desk. The office was silent. The sound of his fingers on the keys travelled easily around the becalmed room. The mouse-click on 'send' was like a fingersnap. Thirty-seven computers chirped nearly simultaneously.

Francis stopped staring at Bob and turned his head to the screen. He opened the email and a rare workplace smile wriggled across his face.

Arthur drives a Lexus SUV. He had an argument with a nice chap at the station and the lining of his Burberry raincoat has a nasty little rip in it. In the light of these developments, today's dilemma is now closed and no further entries can be accepted.

And Bob had put a little smiley at the end of the message. Francis rubbed his index finger over his thumb-nail, trying to determine the significance of this collision of punctuation. He looked around the room – still quiet, still no buzz of workplace conversation, still a tension in the air as though something was unresolved, something could still go either way, no one wanted to be first to laugh or to smile consolingly, to offer to buy the first round tonight, to dole out the manly slap across the shoulder either in solidarity or in hilarity. Then again, thought Francis, half of them are such slow readers that they're probably still processing it.

Bob played the bass at the weekends, he had his midlife-crisis band that booked pubs on quiet nights, brought a few friends, wives and curious acquaintances to the bar, the extra sales more or less exactly covering the extra electricity the band would be pulling through the landlord's meter. Francis had gone once, two years earlier, to hear them grind out classics from the seventies and would-be future classics from current indie-landfill bands. He could have given the band a lift, sprinkled some twinkly keyboard over the lumpen guitar stomp – they would still have been the ones booking the pub, rather than vice versa, but maybe one or two people might have come back after hearing them once. But Francis had never suggested, Bob had never asked, nothing had come of it. Of course, Bob didn't know that Francis played but maybe, just maybe, he should have bothered to find out. Maybe he could have asked Francis about himself for a change rather than giving him the latest despatches from the front-line of hilarity and derring-do that was Bob's life.

Let him get another warning, thought Francis, audibly harrumphing into the remnants of his coffee, then maybe he can get the boot next time there's a redundancy round and we can all get some more work done. After all, it was about time that one of his oh-so-hilarious emails backfired.

Only four months earlier, Steve was excited, he was buying a new car, the first time he had been able to afford a new car, here he was with a proper job and he'd been saving and now he was buying a new car, not too flashy, well, maybe a little bit flashy (but not too much, oh no, or the insurance would be crippling) and he'd chosen the leather seats option so it had to be custom-built, was in the factory this week, he'd have it before the end of the month.

Bob had phoned Steve one day, gone outside, used his mobile, withheld the number, put on a ludicrous estuary-accent and told him the order had been accidentally cancelled but that for a small extra contribution he could have someone else's car, no longer required due to tragedy, never left the parking lot, deluxe, extra features – only one minor snag, left-hand drive. Steve went pink, verging on red and out it all came, the sale of goods act, the contract, the small claims court, not a penny more and must be right-hand drive. So Bob had improvised and said they could have it converted, move the steering wheel and the three pedals but the fourth pedal would be a problem. The fourth pedal repeated a high-pitched, breathless Steve. Yes, the fourth pedal, the pratt pedal. The pratt pedal, what's that for, gasped a panicky Steve. It's for pratts like you, said Bob, in his normal voice, striding back into the room, phone held high, trailing a small coterie, a cabal of Bob-fans. Steve slammed the phone down as the laughter erupted and Arthur came out of his office, smiling, in on the joke and Steve had transferred to another department by the end of the following quarter, all smiles and good humoured and up for a laugh but never having shaken the hunted-deer look from his eyes. It was time something backfired on Bob.

The phone rang, a double-ring – an external call, not one of the lords and masters from upstairs but someone from outside the rarefied atmosphere of the company, a voice of reason and calm – he hungrily seized the handset and drew it to his mouth.

The woman wanted Bob.

Francis looked over at Bob, hunched like a sad-sack over his desk, surely his shoulders weren't heaving, were they? Not worth taking the chance, thought Francis, better to act professionally, may I ask who's calling, may I take a message, may I help in any way? Yes, I work with Bob; yes we work on the same systems; yes, we have had the same training; yes, we're the same seniority; yes, yes, yes

I am interested in working for your client; yes, I can find a quiet place for a telephone interview in a half-hour.

Yes, if I resign today, I could start at your client's company in twenty-eight days.

You snoozed, Bob, and you lost.

Twenty-five minutes later, carrying a notebook and a pen, leaving his jacket over his chair, Francis calmly stood up and walked towards the door. His gait was uncomfortable, his legs had forgotten how to walk naturally and so he was left striding woodenly, as though in a pastiche of normal graceful, relaxed walking – he looked like a man trying to hide the fact that he was excited about where he was going, even though he was going to the uncomfortably small, windowless meeting room two floors down which no one ever booked and which, according to the browser-based room booking system which had replaced Angie and a diary eighteen months earlier, was vacant from then until armageddon. The jacket over the chair would show he wouldn't be out for long, the stationery would show he was going to a meeting, the notebook already had a first draft of his letter of resignation.

Thirty-five minutes later, having been on the phone for twenty-two minutes and spent a few minutes composing himself in the underused and poorly ventilated toilets on the same floor as the meeting room, Francis returned to his desk, dropped his notebook with a surprisingly loud slap, causing heads to twitch around, which he did not even acknowledge as he was about to knock on Arthur's door. He hadn't bothered to find an envelope – what would have been the point?

"How can I help you, Francis?"   Arthur was smiling warmly, gesturing to the chair he wanted Francis to sink into, where he could take a load off, showing that he had the time and the inclination to listen and to discuss, showing that he was responsible for his underlings' pastoral care, not just promotions, pay-rises and annual performance reviews.

Francis felt awkward, his hand shook ever so slightly, the movement amplified by the flapping paper as he stepped over to the desk, tried to place it into Arthur's hand but Arthur did not have his hand up to receive it so Francis placed it on the desk in front of him. "I just wanted to give you this."

"What's this about?" Arthur sounded concerned, he tried a half-smile, he looked down, the smile faded. "Oh Francis."

"Yes, I'm afraid so. It's time. Frankly, I've had enough. Even if there wasn't something else to go to, I need to get out of here. I'm... I'm... I'm dying here, Arthur. I'm suffocating. I'm drowning."

"For goodness sake, man, pick one metaphor at a time."

"And it's comments like that, from people like you with your rude Lexus driving and your good university education, mocking people like me and my red-brick university... Anyway, adios."

Francis turned to the door.

"Really? Adios? Firstly, have you forgotten your notice period and secondly, have I really been such an awful person to work for that you have nothing else to say to me?"

Francis turned back.

"Of course you haven't been an awful person, Arthur. You're just weak, you don't stand up for your staff, you agree ridiculous deadlines before talking to the people who will actually do the work, then just look at us with those pleading eyes because your bonus depends on it but obviously our bonuses don't because you set them and there's nothing left in the pot once you've stuck your snout in. I don't know what you do in this comfortable little office but it sure as hell isn't making the work any easier on the other side of your goldfish-bowl window and maybe, just for once, you could leave your door open and listen and actually understand what your team does all day."

He took a deep breath, put his hand on his chest, closed his eyes for a few seconds, using the inner-calm technique from the book his sister had given him the previous Christmas. He opened his eyes and continued, Arthur not having filled the gap. "I can work my notice period, but don't expect me to do anything. I won't need a reference, just written confirmation of my dates here, which is all this company does anyway. So, I'll be occupying that chair for the next four weeks. But I really don't have anything else to say. And I've got a headache coming on so I think I'll go home now."

Francis turned back to the door, opened it, walked out of the room. Now his legs knew how to relax into their stride. He slung his jacket over his arm, picked up his bag, took his wallet from his drawer and left the room.

Arthur opened the door to his office, walked over to Bob's desk, took his wallet from his pocket, extracted a crisp ten pound note and slapped it down on the desk.

"You're going to have to tell me how you got him to do that. And why does he think I drive a Lexus? Doesn't everyone know I cycle to the station?"

Soft Shoe Kick

For a man who looked down, who regularly found what others had lost, as well as studying the litter sprinkled and cast around, Paul tripped over surprisingly often. The grazed knees from tumbles had given way to stubbed toes from stumbles as he left his teenage years behind – but his mother had never understood how a boy could miss the paving slab at a jaunty angle, the imperfectly aligned inspection cover (or manhole cover as she still called them), the dip behind the kerb, the straggling thorny bramble branch – all of them conspiring to throw her clumsy son to the ground.

The downward-looking gait had come from Paul's father, a man who had reunited many a happy stranger with his property, who only sought the reward of knowing he had done the right thing. Paul had watched from behind the bannister of the stairs when one such relieved man had come to the door – his father had found a wallet in the park, in the long grass, goodness knows how he had spotted it, and had carefully looked through it, found a name, but not an address, gone to the telephone directory and, eventually and after many right-named wrong numbers, had found the rightful owner. The owner had smiled, he had offered a bottle, foil covering over a fat neck (his father explaining later about the sparkling drink needing the cage to hold the cork down), but Paul's father had refused and refused kindly, inventing a medical prohibition on alcohol to suggest he was no puritan, no proselytising teetotaller, that he was not at all offended by the offer but insetad compelled to refuse for the good of his health. Paul's father only wanted to know he was helping others, in the hope that they might, perhaps only once, perform an altruistic act of their own and spread the kindness further.

Paul's father was not a clumsy man – how could he be when he studied the ground so carefully? How his son could be so prone to accidents was a mystery he could not solve.

One day Paul spotted a pink slip of paper fluttering along the ground and spiralling in the breeze. It was in the company of a cashpoint receipt, the cellophane from around a cigarette packet, and the top strip torn from a chocolate bar wrapper. They had been dropped only a few yards from a bin. When he was closer, he saw that the slip was white with pink and black print, a lottery ticket, carrying that day's date, for the pan-European draw, a multiple roll-over, a projected nine-figure jackpot, no name or address written on the back. A man or a teenager, hooded, possibly early-twenties, probably younger, was the only person on foot, about a hundred yards away. He was digging through the pocket of his tracksuit, pulling out items of paper, possibly receipts, maybe short affectionate notes from a girlfriend, discarding many to the ground, leaving a trail.

The lottery ticket could be his – or it could have been thrown from a passing car, or dropped by someone else earlier that day. The litter trail from the hooded man did not extend all the way back to Paul. The ticket might prove worthless but that would not be known until that night. He knew the right thing to do.

Carrying the pink scooter, he ran after the hood. Paul had just taken his daughter to the nursery, he preferred to go on foot, the scooter was lighter than the buggy, there were periods when she would propel herself (downhill), kicking the sole of her left soft shoe against the pavement, as well as stretches (uphill, flat, only slightly downhill) when she needed to be towed, both soles resting side by side on the platform – on balance it was less work for him, more fun for her and easier to carry home. It was no inconvenience to catch up with the young man – it was on his way, not that a diversion from his route would have stopped him – it was the right thing to do.

"Excuse me!" No answer, stride unbroken, hands in pockets, the youth continued. "Excuse

me!" Still no response so Paul gently tapped the
fellow on the shoulder and stood back as the kid
whirled around, snarl on his face, earbuds pulled
out, tinny noises now leaking into the air. The
aggression knocked Paul back a step and he tried
desperately not to stare at the criss-cross markings
on the side of the youth's face – it was as though he
had run (or been thrown) into a chicken-wire fence,
or possibly had an argument with a supermarket
basket.

"What?"

"I think you might have dropped something."
This was Paul's standard line. Ask someone if
they've dropped a tenner and they will say yes and
thank you and pocket the money and smirk and
probably tell their friends about the idiot who gave
them free money. Tell someone that you think they
might have dropped something and the person who
dropped the money will look for it, properly search
each pocket, not find it and know what they have
lost and ask for it – anyone else would simply have
to be lucky.

Paul had found an MP3 player on a train once –
he was unfamiliar with its controls but he managed
to find the owner's name, stored within it, displayed
on the screen when the right buttons were pressed
or spun in the right order. He considered the lost-
property department but thought they were
understaffed and overwhelmed and probably
uninterested in proactively finding the owner. He

emailed the manufacturer with the serial number of the machine, telling them he wasn't expecting them to give him the contact details of the owner but that they were welcome to give his details to them – they wrote back that it was unregistered. He put the name into every search engine he could find, harvested email addresses, wrote to each and every one, starting with those who lived in or near his city. He told them that he had found something of theirs and that if they could tell him correctly what it was, he would return it forthwith. Most did not reply, some messages bounced from invalid mailboxes, one gushing reply thanked him and told him how she had lost her purse and told him about the sentimental value of the contents and that she would come to him to collect it and thank you and thank you and he had to write back and say that, sorry, he hadn't actually found a purse. He emailed the lost-property office to ask if anyone had reported the machine lost. They didn't reply. Finally, he took it to them to be filed and stored, the eyes of the man at the desk lit up when he saw the item, we don't get many of these, yes we'll give it back to you if it's not collected within a month – I don't want it, said Paul – that's the policy, said the man. But the following month, when Paul enquired, it had been collected. Paul didn't want it for himself, but he didn't want it to go to the lost-property office man either, the man who didn't look him in the eye, which didn't mean he had stolen it, of course, but Paul was not happy with the outcome. He hadn't wanted the thanks of the rightful owner, he hadn't wanted a reward, he just wanted to know that the right thing had been done.

The reply coming from the face in the hood was startling in its vulgarity, delivered with phlegm and vigour but little wit. The ridged red grid stretched and flexed as the profanities poured out.

"I wasn't accusing you of dropping litter," said Paul, "although you obviously have been. I just thought you might have thrown away something you didn't mean to."

"And?" said the man, stepping towards Paul, shoulders leaning in, hands clenched, head twitching forward.

"And I thought you might want it back," said Paul. "Just check if there's anything missing and, if it's what I've found, I'll give it back to you."

"What have you found?"

"Well if I tell you that, you'll... you might... well, most people, would just say it was theirs so they could have it."

"Cut the crap man and hand it over. Gimme my tenner."

"It's not a tenner."

"Twenty?"

"No."

"It's too early for this. If you'd tried this later, I'd've taken twenty off you, maybe your phone too. But right now, just go away. Okay?"

Paul turned around, without saying another word and walked away, carried on walking until his heart rate reduced, walked a mile away from home, having gone the wrong way because the alternative would have been to have walked alongside, or in front of, or behind, the youth that he had tried to help, who had repaid him with threats of violence and the suggestion that he would have been mugged if only the youth could have been bothered to make the effort. Surely no one gets mugged before 9am while carrying a child's pink scooter?

That night, the pink slip became worth a nine-figure sum. Paul was unsure how to proceed. It was his duty to hand in the ticket, to explain the circumstances, to let the process run, to hope that no one would claim the prize, that the lottery investigation would find no other possible recipient, that the lottery regulations, and the discretion of the board, would lead to his receiving the single largest jackpot paid in the country. There was only one winning ticket, the prize would not be shared. Or maybe the rightful owner would turn up and, of his own volition, give Paul a finder's fee – even one hundredth of the prize would change his life forever. Or maybe the rightful owner would turn up, collect his prize and enjoy it all himself.

Paul's father would have known what to do – he would have immediately surrendered the ticket, described clearly and carefully where he had found it, contacted the local press to give the rightful owner the greatest chance of receiving this frankly inconceivable amount of money. He would have refused any finder's fee, he would even have kept his own name out of the paper. He wouldn't have needed the thanks or the reward or the fame.

Or would he? Paul's father might have turned down a bottle of fizz, even if it was the finest champagne because, as he put it himself that night, even the best champagne will be nothing but a wooziness and a headache by the following morning – but would he have turned down a seven-figure thank-you cheque from a man who would have considered that nothing but small change?

Paul picked up the phone, started pressing the buttons, then stopped. He could not ask his father for advice this time. Either his father would tell him to give up the money, even to refuse the prize if subsequently awarded to him when all other avenues were exhausted, in which case, if he followed the advice, he would have to live with the knowledge that providence (or random chance, as he preferred to think of it) had offered him a risk-free ladder to a life comfortable beyond his comprehension and he had pushed it aside in favour of pride and a hairshirt which would grow itchy beyond what he could bear in a matter of hours – or alternatively his father would tell him to keep the money, in which case his opinion of his father, the incorruptible man, the moral compass, the paragon, would be be dented, an ugly scratch ground into its highly polished surface, his father shown to be, like everyone else, a man who had his price, even though that price was significantly higher than that of most.

He should keep the money for his daughter. But did she need so very much? Were they poor without this? Would it make them happy? Would it make them happy if he was sent to prison – he was searching the news to find out what others had done and he found no stories of people winning vast sums from finding winning tickets and being awarded the prizes. The legitimate owners could give their lottery numbers, the date and time and place of purchase – even without their name and address on the back they could prove it was theirs and thus the finder, passing the ticket off as his own, without any knowledge of the place of purchase, could be easily unmasked and prosecuted for theft. Was he prepared to risk everything? Then again, if one were to gamble such high stakes as one's own freedom, would the prize of over one hundred million pounds be sufficient incentive as against the low chance of being caught?

The ticket was a 'lucky dip' – a random set of numbers generated by the till thus reducing the possibility that the rightful owner would know the numbers, thus reducing the chance that they would know they had won, thus reducing the chance that they would make a ticketless claim for the jackpot, thus reducing the chance that he could be caught.

It nagged at him. He did not discuss it with his wife – she abhorred the lottery, would not condone his gambling on it, would not buy tickets for others with their own money, would not collect even the smallest prizes on behalf of friends or elderly relatives who gave her a wink and told her to spend the money on something for the child – a chocolate something and a toy and maybe a book.

And, if he discussed it with her, he would have to tell her about the youth in the hood, the confrontation, the violence in the man's eyes, the angle of his torso, all threat-jut and macho-pose, the language – well, actually the language was quite funny out of context, after the fact, without the smell of the man standing too close – his desperation with his pathetic life plainly so very near the surface – maybe one day he'll try to mug someone and the sadness will be overbearing and he'll weep at the absurdity of it all and his nearly-victim will put an arm around him and there-there him and they'll share a moment before the thug shakes him off and maybe slaps him across the shoulder, which they'll both know he doesn't mean but has to perform, to keep up appearances, to put the earth back onto its usual axis, and with a sneer and a noisy, hacking phlegmy spit, he'll be gone back into his subway where, for all Paul knows, he lives.

He put the lottery ticket into his book, not as a bookmark, not sticking out where someone (his wife) might see it, but fully concealed, hard against the spine, marking a page he has already read so that it could not fall out unexpectedly as he turned a page while reading a little before going to sleep, so that his wife would not have to see the fluttering and would not have to reach forward to see what caused it and would not have to ask him why he's been wasting his money on this gambling.

In the middle of the following week, he saw the youth again, this time from across the road. He was talking to a policeman – well, not a real policeman, according to Paul, but one of those pretend policemen who can't really do much except turn up and tut and then wait for a proper officer to come along if tutting doesn't solve the problem, doesn't stop the rumble, won't placate the crowd. They seemed to be sharing a joke, and a see-ya-later and then they were off going their separate ways and Paul hurried past and wished that the pink scooter wasn't quite so bright and distinctive and attention-grabbing.

"Sorry about last week."

Paul turned. The youth was standing in front of him, wringing his hands, looking at his feet, then looking up with an attempt at a placatory smile.

"I was out of order. I was thinking about it on the way home. Thank you for asking but I hadn't dropped anything – must have been someone else. And I don't nick people's phones – not any more, not after I got this." He gestured at his marked face.

"And not after I met Stevie." He pointed to the pretend-policeman slowly walking away, nodding to the passersby who all seemed to ignore him. "Not like that, just met him when he nicked me and we got chatting and he's trying to help me turn things around."

Paul nodded, managed a slight smile. "Well thank you for saying all that. I appreciate it – last week it made me quite nervous about doing my normal walk – but not any more. I'm Paul, by the way."

"Mark."

Paul offered his hand which Mark slowly reached out to take and to shake in a weak, desperate to pull back, handshake.

"What was it you found? Just out of interest."

"Lottery ticket."

"Worth anything?"

"Find out tonight." Paul immediately regretted this reply. He could have said it turned out to have been a couple of weeks old and matched no numbers and he'd thrown it away. That would have been a lie of closure, if he'd delivered it calmly and dismissively. Instead his lie needed a second act, the next time he met Mark, he was bound to be asked again. What would he tell him? Maybe say it won a tenner and offer him half? That would probably do – Mark would be happy with a few quid for nothing more than asking (a bit like mugging but without even needing to threaten, or to carry out, violence) and they could move on.

"Split any prize?" asked Mark, clearly thinking he was donning a cheeky grin, rather than the haunted spectre of ruined teeth inside chapped lips.

"Why not?" said Paul, his own smile little better than Mark's. "If we're incredibly lucky that might even be five quid each."

"What numbers we got?"

"I can't remember."

"Let's see the ticket – I want to know tonight how much you're going to owe me."

"I don't have it here – left it on the hall table." Why had he lied about that? He didn't even have a hall table and what was wrong about saying it was in his book? Had he really thought he would sound like a snob if he owned up to reading? Was he assuming that Mark didn't (couldn't?) read and would be somehow insulted. Paul realised that was precisely what was subconsciously running through his head. "And it was someone else's choice, so it's not like the numbers are going to mean anything to me. Actually, I think it was a lucky dip."

"That's good," said Mark, nodding. "Less chance that the guy who lost it will have any idea that we owe him a tenner. Or more, after all, it could be you."

"Us!" said Paul, smiling his fake smile again. "Anyway, gotta go. See you around – I'll give you your share next time I see you. Although half of zero..."

Paul's original intention had been to hold onto the ticket for a little while – after all, he had six months to claim the prize – see whether the news would report a sob story about some idiot who knew he had won a vast fortune but had lost the ticket, then maybe wait to see whether the loser-winner offered a reward, then maybe wait to see if the reward was increased.   He was expecting nothing, that the rightful owner would know nothing, that after maybe three months he could cash it in. His second exchange with Mark had unnerved him more than he thought it should – after all, there was now one fewer person likely to attack him in the street, mere days after he thought there was one person very likely to attack him in the street. He realised that he was a worse judge of character than he thought, or that people could continually surprise him with their action, and the sooner he had the money tucked away safely in a bank account, the better. He had decided that leaving the ticket at home (at risk of burglary) was better than carrying it with him (at risk of pick-pocketing, mugging, loss, water damage from rain or from sweat or from a child's waterpistol). But now safely depositing the money in a bank (at risk of identity fraud, collapse of financial institution, national economy going down the tubes) seemed the best option.

Where could he deposit such a vast sum? The people at the lottery would probably be able to help him. He phoned the office, put on his best sorry-for-himself sniffle and said he wasn't feeling up to going into work that day. He picked up his book, flicked through to check the ticket was there, put it back in the book, gripped it tightly, the white knuckles the only sign that he was holding it too tightly, too desperately. He went out of the house, locked the door then stopped, turned, opened the door, went in, walked into the kitchen, took the ticket out and laid it on the counter. He looked at it. He breathed deeply, he turned it over and, with the wonderful permanence of cheap biro ink, he carefully and clearly wrote his name and address in block capitals on the reverse. He locked the door behind him, thus protecting his family's small collection of not particularly valuable possessions.

It was another six days before Paul met Mark again, six days of little white lies while he thought about how to tell his family, six days of being officially too sick to go to work (well, four working days and the two of the weekend), six days of letting the answerphone take the calls from the financial advisers – he had agreed to talk to them but had failed to appreciate the effort they would expend to hook a client as good and as green as him. Six days of trying to act normal (whatever that was), keep the hiding-something smile from the corners of his mouth.

He was on his way back from the nursery, walking through the subway, pink scooter over his shoulder when he heard someone running to catch up.

"Hey, mate, damn it, forgotten your name."

"It's Paul. Hello Mark."

"Just wondered how much we won."

"Was a good one, Mark. We didn't just match three and win ten pounds. We matched four."

"Four?! What's that – a few grand?"

"Nowhere near."

"A few hundred?"

"Forty."

"Forty! You're messing with me. It's got to be worth more than forty."

"Surprised me too but there it is. I've got your twenty here. How d'you want it? Two tens okay with you?"

"You're lying to me. I know you won more than that. Must have been quite a bit more if you're so happy to give twenty quid away."

"Mark – that's what you get for four numbers. I'm sorry it's not more."

"Do not mess with me. I used to do this for a living. I used to knock over little clever people like you and I'd know when they were hiding some more notes, I could see it in their eyes and smell it in their sweat. When someone as tight as you hands over anything that quickly, there's more to be had."

"Mark, I really don't..."

"So here's what we do. You give me all the money you've got. I go home and check what four numbers won. Then I give you your change next time I see you. Or you better be carrying the rest if I'm still short. You get me?"

"No."

"Smart boy like you not get me?"

"I understand what you're saying but I'm not giving you anything more than these two notes as per our agreement."

"Ooh! As per! Get your wallet out again and empty it. You've seen these scars, you can't stop looking at them, you know I can handle myself."

"Actually, those scars make me think you can't handle yourself."

"Price just went up, Paulie. Get your phone out too."

"Mark, this isn't funny."

"You're right it isn't."

Over Mark's shoulder, Paul could see the policeman, Stevie, walking towards them. He was walking back to his office, probably looking forward to a cup of tea, maybe a muffin. Not many other people walked through this subway which joined two dead-ends that had probably been a single street before being sliced apart by the bypass. The police used it, Mark used it and Paul insisted that he would not be too scared to use it – but not many others went near. Not many other people walked anywhere anyway.

"You all right, Mark?" asked Stevie as he passed.

"Fine, mate." Mark stared hard at Paul but Paul just calmly looked straight back. He said nothing, he did nothing.

"Still on for the pub tonight – around eight?"

"Fine, see you there." Mark hadn't taken his eyes off Paul as Stevie moved past, the pull of the early-morning snack stronger than the wish to be sociable.

They said nothing until Stevie was long out of the subway and probably sitting with his feet up on his desk.

"Why didn't you say anything to him?"

"Because I reckoned I could take you."

And, before he'd even finished the sentence, Paul did.

Insofar as Paul thought about it at all, rather than just relying on instinct and reflex and pure animal hatred, he knew that the money in his pocket (maybe about fifty pounds) was a woefully insignificant and frankly unnoticeable fraction of his total worth. It was not the point – he wanted to do the right thing, to finish the rehabilitation of this feral creature that had been started by the chicken-wire fence (or possibly the shopping basket), to make the streets just a little bit safer for everyone, even if not a place where they could drop their valuables and be wholly confident they would be returned.

The more he worked, the more the youth in the hood became the embodiment of everything that was or ever had been wrong: the boys who laughed at his polyester jacket when he entered the sixth form, the climate change agnostics who felt that

near-total scientific consent was invalid because it
was only near-total, the pitying look in the face of
the girl who did not want to go on a date with him,
the drivers barrelling along the road yap-yap-
yapping into their mobile phones and never being
stopped, never mind prosecuted, the irritating bark
of the dog next door, identikit suburban wives in
year-round sunglasses, the charming and friendly
interviewer who didn't offer him a job, the pile of
rubbish in the loft that he couldn't bring himself to
sort through or to throw out, people who dropped
litter, people who shouted at their children in public
places, people who didn't control their children in
public places, people who led their countries into
war, people who tried to justify the people who led
their countries into war, ill-informed journalists
filling their readers with falsehood and bile,
talentless tabloid-created celebrities, people making
themselves rich from socially useless activities,
advertising, odd flavours of crisps and endless lists
passing themselves off as incisive prose.

He swung the scooter into the man's head, beat
him to the ground and carried on swinging it over
and over until his hand grew tired and so he kicked
him instead, swinging his soft canvas shoes into the
tensed and writhing torso and head and abdomen
until it was limp and the kicks only caused ripples in
the flesh but no other movement. His toes hurt the
way they did when he stubbed them on the dining
table, the way they did when he caught them on a

raised paving slab and stumbled and nearly fell. Finally it was enough, he dropped the spattered and deformed scooter and walked away, out of the subway, past the fire station, past the office of the police community support officers (safe neighbourhood team) and on and on until his shoes had stopped dribbling a trail along the pavement and he reached home and he walked into the hall, through into the kitchen, took a black plastic sack, emptied his pockets then stuffed all his clothes, even his underwear, into the sack and dropped it on the floor. Onwards to the bathroom where, under a hot shower, he washed every last trace, scrubbing under his nails, clawing the shampoo into and out of his hair. He cut his nails, then brushed under them again.

The black plastic sack went into the cupboard under the sink in the bathroom – he'd worry about it tomorrow, split the contents between a few bins or maybe take a trip out to the tip. He dressed smartly. He shaved. He called the office, he was feeling better but then the train had been cancelled, he had started feeling faint, he had had a little rest, he was coming into work now, sorry he's going to be late, sorry, sorry, see you later. Sorry, goodbye.

Stevie had seen him. He had a little over one hundred and seventeen million pounds in a bank account. He could afford to collect his daughter by car that afternoon. He had had his back to Stevie. He would never wear those clothes again. They would soon be living in a new neighbourhood, just as soon as he could bring himself to tell his wife.

Two Sole Certainties

The problem with tax is that it simultaneously bores and enrages people, so bear with me while I get through the boring bit and arrive at the part where you start grinding your teeth, chewing your nails, tearing your hair out and any other cliché you care to mention.

Big people don't pay tax, neither do big corporations – this may be a commonly held view but it's overly simplistic. Of course they pay tax – they just don't pay it at the same proportion as a little person like you. Or me. Or that guy over there. Why is this? Well, they pay (a smaller) something else to someone else instead – they pay the tax lawyer and they pay the tax accountant and those two charming characters find ways around the requirement to help fund the country.

This is sometimes the point where people get angry. Ah, say the captains of industry, but we employ people and we pay enough in tax without having to part with the full 50% of all earnings above whatever it is.   Besides, they say, the government will only waste it.

The way the rich rail against paying their share – you'd think they were suffering the way that Queen suffered in the early years (that's the band, not the monarch.) Around the time of their third album, the band members noticed that their managers were still paying them £60 per week. Freddie was being told he couldn't have a piano (but that they could rent him one). Roger was being asked to stop hitting the drums so hard because he kept breaking drumsticks and replacing them, apparently, was an unbearable expense. Certainly no one would have stumped up to buy Brian a new fireplace (you'll have to figure that reference out for yourselves). The managers of the record company were simultaneously doing things like buying their third Rolls Royce or installing more swimming pools in their homes. The penny dropped (or rather, the pennies weren't dropping, ha ha) and the band began a lengthy process of extracting themselves from this exploitative situation.

Those complaining about the very notion of paying normal tax are acting as though, were they to pay their full share, they would be the ones earning £60 per week while the government would be swanning around in Rolls-Royce cars when it wasn't pampering itself in one of its many swimming pools. Clearly the proportions are not anywhere near as gruelling but, to the tax protesters, anything higher than zero taxation appears to be an indignity up with which they can not (and will not) put.

I wonder whether they've really thought this through because, to put it in their terms, they could consider the United Kingdom to be a massive venture-capital organisation. The country puts up the money for each and every one of us – it takes the colossal financial risk of education, health-care, roads, telecoms, airports, railways, utilities, etc, etc for each and every one of us. The reason it takes the risk is because, like any good venture-capitalist, it expects some of its investments to repay big-time and that this will more than cancel out the money lost to the sloths, the ne'er-do-wells, the lazy and the frankly rubbish.

A country can't act as ruthlessly as a venture-capitalist though – it can't drop the people who aren't going to bring in massive profits – it has to look after us from cradle to grave. And in order for this to work, for society to function, the rich must pay their taxes properly – they must subsidise everyone else – that's how they pay back the huge investment that was made in them and how they ensure that future generations can also benefit from a similar investment.

How long would venture-capital funds last if the successful businesses could simply run away and hide in a foreign country, continue to pull in large sums of money but refuse to hand over the agreed percentage? How long can nations function in any meaningful sense if they keep providing hiding places for the rich to stash their money and then acting like they can't see it?

The time for tax loopholes has ended. In the past, there has been no political will to close them but now it will have to happen. Because now the little people can put their noses in the trough too or, to use a better analogy, can swat the government away from drinking their blood the same way the big boys do. It's all there, as clear as tax legislation can be (which, admittedly is not very clear at all). The twists and turns that have sheltered the (sometimes ill-gotten) gains of the soi-disant elite can be used by every dustman, nurse, teaching assistant, washing machine repairman, chartered surveyor – everyone can have a little more money in their pocket.

Obviously this won't last long. Once enough of us are doing this, the law will be changed – it will have to be changed – and the big fish will be swept up in the net just like everyone else. So sign up now and make a few quid before the brave new world of proper taxation for all begins.

Click _here_ to find out how it works, explained quickly and simply – well, as quickly and simply as I could, given the subject matter.

Benjamin Franklin told us that nothing can be said to be certain, except death and taxes. For you, dear reader, temporarily at least, I can help reduce your taxes. I can't help you with the death part.

12 March 2011, 5.17pm

I've had no hits on my previous posting to this blog. I've tweeted about it too: "How to legally shirk tax like the big boys: http://j.mp/f1hfc4 – sign up now, risk free!" But as no one follows me (how do you get followers, short of being on the telly?), it's hard to know whether anyone's even read it.

It won't be surprising to read, therefore, that no one has signed up for the scheme – which is a shame because it does need at least twenty-seven people on board for the savings to cancel out the start-up costs. Have emailed everyone I know and asked them to circulate it. I've put it on Facebook but that was a dead loss too. Are my friends too old? Should I cultivate the friendship of students – although they don't pay tax so they're a fat lot of use.

15 March 2011, 4.23pm

George The Ginger Rodent has signed up! I'm not sure he's a real person though as he gives his email address as george@gingerrodent.com. I haven't tried emailing him but, given that the domain 'gingerrodent.com' is available for purchase, I'd hazard a guess that the email address is bogus.

15 March 2011, 4.47pm

I'm not going to apologise for doubting you, George, and I would be grateful if you would avoid that sort of language. I just emailed you and my message bounced so I repeat – that email address is bogus and you are soiling my blog with your puerile nonsense.

The question remains – how do I get more exposure for my grand scheme?

15 March 2011, 5.07pm

I shall rewrite my original blog post and offer it to the quality newspapers. Surely one of them will be interested – frankly, even if it just appears on one of their websites rather than in a 'proper' paper, that ought to generate some interest. Tipping point of 27 people – how hard can it be? And once we get started, those 27 people will be blabbing it around and we'll really take off.

19 March 2011, 10.34am

I can't believe they've all turned me down – they can't have properly read my piece. I say they've all turned me down – obviously not all of them bothered to reply but I think I can assume that silence is equivalent to lack of interest.

If I can escape moderation, I could post a potted

summary to the comments section under any news story regarding tax, together with a link to my site – instead of getting my full article into the paper. If I sprinkle that around a few different sites, I ought to get a hit rate spike.

19 March 2011, 6.21pm

Hit rate has gone through the roof. But no one is signing up. Strange.

19 March 2011, 7.05pm

Damn and blast it! When I went in to remove all traces of the ginger rodent, I must have polluted the link to the email address. Not entirely sure how that could have happened as they're in different sections of the web form. Never mind – have corrected it now.

19 March 2011, 7.12pm

Hit rate fallen to zero. Not nearly zero – actually zero. A war of moderation has been declared against my postings to newspapers' comments boards. Not a single one is remaining. Wow – when they wake up, they really get going.

Back to the drawing board.

20 March 2011, 1.07am

Three word comment posted to my previous blog entry. "Cease and desist". Hmm. Another crank – maybe a disgruntled tax lawyer, annoyed that a 'civilian' such as myself has the ability, temerity and bare-faced cheek to try to figure out this putrid number-crunching system without paying a stipend to him or one of his ilk.

Cease and desist? I shall do no such thing and here's why. I have discovered that the costs of setting up the off-shore company are smaller than I expected so I shall get the ball rolling while I wait. Yes, good people, I am putting my money where my blog-typing fingers are. This will mean absolutely no start-up costs for any of you lot – instead I'll have first dibs on the filthy lucre to recoup my expenses. That ought to mean little more than you waiting a week or so to get the last few pennies from your first pay cheques.

20 March 2011, 3.43am

Blasted wireless router connection kept dropping at inconvenient moments. Have just spent thirty-seven minutes digging through my cable boxes to find the dark blue lead. Will now be lying on belly on the floor in the corner of the room with the laptop plugged straight into cable modem. That ought to sort the problem.

20 March 2011, 5.07am

A lesser mortal would think there's some sort of conspiracy afoot to prevent my scheme taking off. It turns out that it wasn't the router after all but the connection to the internet that kept dropping, which is strange as earlier I'm sure the laptop wasn't able to connect to the router – not that it could connect to the router but couldn't get out to the internet.

Anyway, enough of the techno-babble. Maybe the machines are always this blasted in the small hours. I'll shut it all down and hope it's in a better mood when I wake up in the morning (or afternoon).

20 March 2011, 11.36am

In case you're wondering about my ability to post these blog entries despite internet problems – there's a world of difference between posting these journal entries during the odd few minutes of connectivity and navigating through complex and potentially financially disastrous web forms. When you've been disconnected and reconnected multiple times, you might be happy to write your thoughts to an (unread) blog and yet still be twitchy about committing to legally binding agreements with organisations (who need credit card numbers and bank details) when you're not convinced that you didn't miss something during a disconnection.

I'm sorry – I said that I was done with the techno-babble. I just didn't want to be criticised by a ginger rodent (or any of his friends) for perceived technical incompetence. I'm not claiming to be a web guru, but I have found a wonderful tax loophole which I invite each and every citizen of Britain to join me in exploiting. Where are you all?

24 March 2011, 7.23pm

I've created a new account with the online newspapers and, rather more subtly than before, posted to discussions under their tax stories, together with a different shortened link to the sign-up page. We'll see how long that ruse works.

24 March 2011, 10.13pm

I can't believe how quickly these people move in and delete my comments. I'd insert rude words at this point if it wasn't for my utter determination to keep my language fit for anyone of any level of sensitivity. Let's just agree that there was some implied swearing and I now feel, for a very short amount of time, very slightly better.

27 March 2011, 3.24pm

Very strange day. A man in sunglasses and what looked a lot like an ear-piece has been following me. I first noticed him across the aisle in the supermarket and just assumed he was a very badly disguised security guard. However, I then noticed him in the health-food shop. Okay, I thought to myself, maybe he's employed by the shopping centre. But, when he was five people behind me in the queue at the post office (out the shopping centre, turn left, walk a few minutes down the street) and, finally, getting into a car parked within sight of mine, I began to wonder what was going on.

I turned into my driveway and he drove past, seeming not to be looking my way. But then maybe he doesn't need to stop because there's a car parked just across the road with someone sitting in it, doing nothing. He's not moving, he's not looking at me, he's just staring straight ahead as though he's listening to the radio. Let's hope he's listening to the radio. I really need him to just be listening to the radio.

27 March 2011, 8.12pm

That must be one hell of an interesting programme on the radio. I wonder if he can see me looking out through the crack in the curtains. I wonder if I should call the police – does it count as harassment, or stalking or an infringement of my civil liberties? Are people allowed to just park their cars and sit doing nothing? Has anyone actually bothered me? What would I be expecting the police to do?

27 March 2011, 10.10pm

Thank you to StJohnsWort for posting the message of support. I'm sorry to hear that you're not in work – mostly sorry to hear of your own reduced circumstances but also, slightly, because it means you can't join my scheme – which is a shame because you're the first person, other than George (and he was just a rodent) to contact me.

Anyway, thank you for advising me to hold on in there and not to let them grind me down (whoever 'them' might be). However, I probably won't take your advice to call the police because I still feel that they'll wonder why I'm calling them and what they're supposed to do about it. And because the car has gone.

Yes, that's right, fans and Worts. The spookily unnerving car and its driver have gone. It is quite dark out there so he could have merely parked slightly further up the street or been replaced by the person on the next shift. Finding myself writing that makes me think I'm being paranoid. And writing *that* reminds me of the hilarious one-liner that, just because you're being paranoid, it doesn't mean that they aren't out to get you.

Somehow, tonight, that's not making me laugh.

27 March 2011, 10.30pm

Just wondered if he's jamming my wireless

connection whenever I start doing something towards setting up the project. And that's got me wondering whether he's StJohnsWort – which is not a healthy state of mind to be in. I'm going to bed – everything seems brighter and happier in daylight. Except, perhaps, victims of bad plastic surgery.

27 March 2011, 11.03pm

Maybe Mr Cease&Desist and the man in the car, and the earpiece man in the shops are all working together. MI5? It surprises me that I'm even writing that but aren't they responsible for the well-being of the homeland? Wouldn't a genius tax avoidance programme (that would either lead to a dramatic reduction in revenue or the need to clamp down on loopholes enjoyed by those who fund the major political parties) count as something that could be bad for the status quo, rank as that status quo might be? Would that fall within their remit?

Well, I ask that question in the hope that someone might answer it tonight, right here, on this blog, while I toss and turn on my bed and hope for sleep, rather than a long-lasting feeling of unease.

28 March 2011, 3.33am

No response yet. 3.30am seemed a good target to aim for – in the hope I would fall asleep and sail merrily past it on the good ship land-of-nod. Sadly,

I didn't and I haven't so here I am checking for replies and finding none. Come on, spooks. Maybe I had subconsciously worked out who was following me when I described the car as spookily unnerving earlier tonight.

Assuming I'm correct, which I admit is fairly unlikely, but – worst case scenario – let's say that I'm being monitored by MI5 as a potential threat to national security, then the obvious question is why am I still able to record my experiences and put them up on the world wide web for all to see?

It could be because no one is reading this so it's no threat – although if that were the case, why would anyone be bothering to follow and monitor me?

28 March 2011, 7.08am

The phone rang twice, then stopped. Three minutes later it rang three times, then stopped. Twenty minutes later it rang once, then stopped. Too early for telemarketing. Too consistent for a wrong number – incompetent diallers need someone to answer to discover that they have dialled incorrectly.

I have unplugged the phone. I'm switching the mobile to silent mode in the hope that I might catch up on some sleep. I'm sure much of this paranoia is derived from sleep deprivation.

28 March 2011, 10.56am

The postman knocked at 10.30am – it surprises me just how often he manages to come exactly on the half-hour – and not just any half-hour but specifically that one. How can he time his walk to such a degree of accuracy? What about parcels for other houses – the times when he needs to knock and wait and wonder whether it can be left safely outside or whether it's worth trying the neighbour or whether he should fill in the "while you were out" card and, if so, whether his pen will have dried up, whether shaking it or blowing onto it or just scribbling it around will get it flowing again.

Then again, I probably only notice when he arrives at 10.30am and ignore any days when he's early or late – the same way that I find it striking how often I look at the clock and it's showing 12.34pm (or, late nights becoming more frequent, 12.34am) while conveniently forgetting that it's a hell of a lot more common for it to be showing a different time.

But I digress. He had a thick envelope, carrying rather more hefty postage than a large-letter stamp, I can tell you. Fortunately, no excess to pay – although, on the odd occasion when a frankly (geddit?) incompetent correspondent underpays, my dear postman normally just shoves it through the letterbox with nary a care in the world. Maybe I'm too British about the whole thing but, much as I would love to reward him for saving me a few pennies from time to time (and saving himself the bother of collecting said pennies), I find myself unable to give him a Christmas box. Just writing the phrase makes me feel like a throwback to 1950s Britain although I have no idea of the more happening nomenclature that the effortlessly trendy would use (not that such people would tip the postman). Either he doesn't call, or I'm not in, or he does call when I'm in but he's so damned efficient that he's gone before I can even think that I need to ask him to wait while I get him the coins to buy a drink, or the note to buy a round. Somehow it never occurs to me to leave the money by the door, nor does it occur to me to just post it to him – the one occasion when no one needs to worry about the urban myth of the postman stealing money from the envelopes because it would be for him anyway – and I don't believe for a minute that they do it, I hasten to add, just in case my postman is reading this blog. In case you are, sir, thank you for the excellent service you provide – the lack of any seasonal gift from me is not a result of stinginess or dissatisfaction, as I hope you now appreciate if you managed to wade through this paragraph which, looking back on it, makes me wish for the services of a good editor who would probably strike the whole thing through for being irrelevant.

I was waffling on mainly because I wasn't looking forward to writing the next paragraph.

The envelope contained The Taxation (International and Other Provisions) Act 2010, together with The Corporation Tax Act 2010 and The Income Tax Act 2007 (ITA) – or at least that was what it appeared to be at first glance. Opening these beautifully bound and pleasingly substantial documents, I had a "Shining" moment when I realised that, instead of being full of lengthy incomprehensible legalistic tax prose, it was in fact made up of lengthy incomprehensible paragraphs of prose written by me. Someone had taken the trouble of printing, many times over, a number of short stories which I have been writing sporadically over the last few years. These stories are, mostly, works of fiction. To be honest, I hadn't quite worked out what to do with them, having not moved beyond the rather sophomoric idea of binding them together under the title "They All Die At The End".

Receiving this in the post is horrible for two reasons. Firstly, at the very back of the booklet which is not The Income Tax Act 2007 (ITA) is a loose sheet, hilariously printed in deep red, which asks, in large gothic print, whether I would like to "perish by car crash, falling from building, falling into canyon, falling onto railway line, falling down stairs, stabbing with bread knife, smacking around the head, starvation, myocardial infarction or by whatever the hell was supposed to happen to the idiot who walks out of his job". These are, of course, the fates of the characters from my short stories – you probably worked that out for yourselves, I apologise for patronising you. (Looking at the list now, I wonder why I didn't drown anyone – maybe save that for volume two.)

The second reason, as if it wasn't horrible enough to be given a menu of potential deaths to choose between, all of which are culled (ouch!) from my own collection of short stories, is that no one has actually read these stories because they only exist on my computer and on a few printouts scattered around the lounge and wedged into jacket pockets (only in my jackets) or slid into rucksack compartments (but only my rucksack). Where the hell is he getting this?

Can this be taken to the police? Does it count as a death-threat? Is it proof of breaking and entering? Has my tormentor committed an offence under Digital Economy Act 2010? Why am I so calm about this?

28 March 2011, 3.43pm

Still getting no hits on this blog and none on my scheme sign-up pages and yet, bizarre as it sounds, I get the feeling that everything I write is being read somewhere by someone – maybe by the man with the sunglasses and ear-piece, or maybe by one of his colleagues, sitting in a car somewhere, maybe on my street, maybe intercepting the wireless data between my trusty laptop and my long-suffering router.

It's unlikely to be read by the charmless policeman I spoke to at the new-look, swanky and highly fortified police station. He could write a manual on how to be sufficiently curt to strongly encourage people to go away without overdoing it and bringing on an official complaint. To say that he had no interest in what I was telling him would be doing a disservice to those who had no interest. He was actively and strongly uninterested, in fact he was making a point of showing how interested he was in not being interested in taking me seriously.

And the drive home – I'll write about that later – I need to have a little rest.

28 March 2011, 6.12pm

I've gone over it again in my mind and I accept that I probably didn't handle it very well.

I probably shouldn't have tried to put my story in context by explaining that I had found a potentially politically explosive tax loophole which I was trying to use as leverage to force a change in the law. I was trying to show that, while not having broken a single law, I could well have made enemies in high places within the government, within the intelligence services and within major corporations and that therefore the threat was credible. I probably sounded like a nutter and, to be fair, they probably get quite a number of them barrelling through the door and giving the full swivel-eyed show.

I was definitely followed on the way home, the man was practically tailgating me, making no effort to be subtle, every time I looked in my rear-view mirror he was laughing. Several cars driving the other way, driving towards me, I had a good view of their drivers pointing at me – the two gun barrel fingers together, the itchy thumb hammer twitching away. The second or third of them was probably the original sunglasses and ear-piece man, possibly the seventh or eighth as well – I can imagine him doubling back along some side road just so he could spook me again, or maybe he's got a twin in the same line of business.

Reading that last paragraph back was not pleasant – I immediately realised how paranoid and generally crazy I must be sounding but you have to believe that this is really happening. It's happening to me, right now, in the late afternoon of 28 March 2011.

1 April 2011, 3.07am

Thumping coming from downstairs. An odd time of the night for self-assembly furniture, or for putting up shelves. It woke me sufficiently for me to write this but, once the laptop had fully started, the noise abated, leaving me wondering whether I dreamt the whole thing.

I would ask the person downstairs (tomorrow during the daytime, obviously) but I don't know that neighbour and don't really want to make their acquaintance while sounding like I'm complaining. Anyway, all quiet now so back to bed, maybe even to sleep.

1 April 2011, 11.33am

More thumping from downstairs but one can't complain about building work around the middle of the day.

But never mind any of that. I have an email from a tax lawyer – he's read my piece, he's analysed it carefully, he got his dusty tomes down from his dusty shelf and read carefully through the appropriate sentences of dusty law. He agrees with me! He's called Bob! Bob wants in – and he wants to help to set up the corporate structure! I phoned him (partly to reassure myself that he actually exists) to talk about where we go next with this. It turns out he's fairly local and is happy to drop in to see me this afternoon for a tête-à-tête.

I didn't want to put him off (and didn't want to sound like a paranoid nutter) but decided it was only fair to warn him so I told him about the strange phone calls and the odd parcel and the being followed. He seemed completely unconcerned about it all – said he knows his rights under the law and isn't going to be made nervous while going about his legitimate business.   I salute his confidence.

1 April 2011, 3.55pm

Brilliant. The power's gone down. I'm writing this on the laptop which, fortunately, has plenty of charge in it.   I'm getting online through the neighbour's unsecured router as mine has been knocked out by the power cut. I hope they get it sorted – would be nice to make Bob a cup of tea when he gets here – although I guess I could go all old-school and boil the water in a saucepan on the gas hob.

1 April 2011, 3.58pm

Just realised that the power cut has knocked out my flat but not my neighbour's router, which is downstairs, in the same block. Maybe we're on a different circuit.   Is that possible?   Would the builders have bothered to do that?   What would have been the point?

But then what's the alternative?   That someone has disconnected my flat prior to a visit from a tax lawyer (or so he claims) who I've never met before and who I will be letting into my home of my own free will? I'm trying not to think about that cliché from police reports of murder victims – the one about how there was no sign of a struggle in the home because the murderer must have been known to the victim. Maybe the murderer had just phoned up to make an appointment in those cases too.

1 April 2011, 4.01pm

A car has just pulled up outside. A man is getting out – he's got his back to me but I think it's sunglasses and ear-piece man. He's going to find out about Bob. Or maybe he is Bob. He's walking towards my door. I'll post this and put more up later.